Caretaker's Apprentice
Curse of the Pika

by

Karen Lindsey Gillespie

DORRANCE
PUBLISHING CO
EST. 1920
PITTSBURGH, PENNSYLVANIA 15238

Dorrance Publishing Co
585 Alpha Drive
Pittsburgh, PA 15238

Visit our website at www.dorrancebookstore.com

ISBN: 978-1-6491-3836-1
eISBN: 978-1-6491-3997-9

Caretaker's Apprentice
Curse of the Pika

To my husband, Kerry, who has always
believed in my magical abilities,
even when I have not.

Disclaimer

There is a truly magical spot located on the backside of Mount Timpanogos in Provo Canyon, Utah, and while some of the places and scenes in this book may seem vaguely familiar to you, the names of those places have been changed to protect the privacy of the residents. The characters in this novel are fictional. Any resemblance they bear to real life persons is purely coincidental.

Genealogy Chart

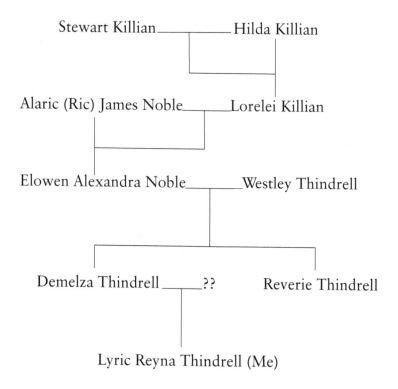

Stewart Killian ———— Hilda Killian

Alaric (Ric) James Noble ——— Lorelei Killian

Elowen Alexandra Noble ——— Westley Thindrell

Demelza Thindrell ___??   Reverie Thindrell

Lyric Reyna Thindrell (Me)

Prologue

"Coming here?" exclaimed the Kitsune over her hibiscus tea, "to live?" A bushy fox tail sprouted and twitched in the chair behind her. Sometimes when she was stressed, she couldn't maintain her human form completely.

"Well, it's just a trial, Allegra, for the summer," responded the young Witch. She had taken great care to lay a proper tea in the library, knowing the ritual would help sooth her territorial and fiercely loyal boarder, and help smooth the way for this unexpected news.

"At least it's a girl and not a boy. Tell me, Reverie, whatever would we do with a loud and messy little boy?" To be fair, she had heard that girls could be loud and messy, too. What an utter nuisance that would be. With that thought, she shot the Witch a panicked glance and a pair of foxy ears covered in rust colored fur with white tufted interiors grew from her head.

Reverie watched the emotions play across the fox woman's face and followed her deliberations with expert dexterity. The Witch replied reassuringly, "Demelza has told me that the girl is quite bright, brilliant even, and quiet, too. She is my niece after all." This last comment she added somewhat proudly.

Allegra made a rude noise, "What would Demelza know? All she thinks about is science. She's always running off all over the world chasing leads and leaving you here to deal with the Mountain. I'll bet the child has never really had a proper mother."

"Allegra," Reverie cautioned quietly, "Mel is my older sister, and I love her despite her single-mindedness. She has her ways of dealing with the Curse, and I have mine."

"*Absent-mindedness* you mean," grumbled Allegra into her tea. Suddenly, a sly thought occurred to her. "Well, look on the bright side, now you will have another Witch to help you with your work." She plucked a cookie from a nearby platter, her ears and tails disappearing as she relaxed and resumed her fully human form.

Reverie bowed her head and smiled into her teacup, knowing she had won the battle. There had never been a downside as far as she was concerned. It was the auburn-headed Kitsune who needed to be convinced of the wisdom of taking in a 13-year-old girl for the summer...maybe longer. Time to drop the other bomb.

"Except, she knows nothing about Witchcraft."

Chapter 1

"Blistering barnacles!" swore Mother with a frustrated sigh. Well, it was as close to swearing as you would get from Mother, but I couldn't blame her; it was taking forever to unload the passengers from the plane. She repeatedly glanced at the time on her phone and jangled her foot nervously.

"It's okay," I assured her with false enthusiasm. I don't know why I always felt it was my job to sooth her, but I did. "I can find baggage claim by myself. You can make your connection to Tokyo if you don't have to go out and come back through security again."

Mother had insisted on accompanying me on the plane from Los Angeles to Salt Lake City even though I told her there was no need to trouble herself because it meant she would end up backtracking. I had flown with her many times before, so I knew the drill, but she said 13 was too young to travel alone. Mother was weirdly old-fashioned about some things.

Our plane was late pushing back from the gate in Los Angeles this morning because a boarding door wouldn't latch properly, so now her time was extremely tight, and there wouldn't be another flight from Salt Lake to Tokyo until tomorrow.

"Thank you, that would be very helpful. I'm expected at the lab in Tokyo tomorrow, and I really need to catch this flight." She sighed with visible relief as we finally started moving down the aisle towards the exit.

"Um...but," I asked nervously, "How will I know her?"

I was meeting my Aunt Reverie, whom I had never laid eyes on. Well, that's not exactly the truth. I knew I had an aunt; she sent me presents for my birthday and Christmas, and I thought I had vague memory of her visiting us once when I was little, but I couldn't remember having any other contact with her.

"That's easy. She'll be the lady who looks exactly like me," she explained with a distracted smile as she patted her very tight, immaculately kept bun of ebony black hair.

My name is Lyric Reyna Thindrell, and I am alone most of the time, if not physically then emotionally. My mother, Dr. Demelza Thindrell, PhD., genius, age 38, obtained a doctorate in genetics and had earned quite the reputation in the scientific community before I was even born. Work and research are her life. Don't get me wrong, I know Mother loves me, and would do anything for me, but she does get rather focused on her job to the detriment of everything else, even, at times, her own well-being.

I've never met my father, and when I ask Mother about him, she is evasive and says he was long gone before I was born. She uses her maiden name, but that doesn't really mean anything. It's quite common nowadays for a woman not to take her husband's name when they marry, especially if she is already a famous scientist, but I know it's naïve to believe they were ever married at all. I know lots of kids whose parents are divorced, but I'm the only person I know who has never met one of their parents. I have considered that perhaps Mother had used less than conventional methods for my conception—she is a geneticist, first and foremost, but I realized there had to have been a lover at some point because those other methods take extensive planning and commitment. I don't think Mother would have ever become pregnant if it had not been an accident. Planning, when it is not related to her research, is not her strong suit.

We exited the jetway and were deposited into the long, wide hallway of the terminal. Mother glanced at the flight board and found her connecting gate located in the opposite direction of baggage claim. "Be safe," she said breezily as she air kissed my cheek and pushed her wire-rimmed glasses up her nose. I knew the lenses were fake because I had tried them on once and had discovered they were just clear glass. She wore them because she thought it made her look older and wiser, and as such, the people in the scientific community would take her work more seriously. "I will call you when I get settled in," she called in parting. Mother doesn't do public displays of emotion. I tried not to get teary eyed as she turned away and sprinted for her gate. She expected me to be brave, and so I took a deep breath and willed the unshed tears away.

When I was very little, there had been a never-ending series of live-in nannies. After I started school, there were teenaged babysitters, overnight summer camps, kind-hearted, elderly neighbors and the dreaded afterschool lessons, so many lessons. There was karate, and choir, and dance, and gymnastics, and you name it, not because I requested, or was interested, or talented, in any of those things, but because Mother thought that they would be good for me, and she could pay someone else to teach me. If she could get me off her hands every day from dawn to dark, she could free up more of her time for her all-consuming, obsessively important work. I think it also made her feel less guilty about leaving me so much.

We tend to move to a different state or country every year or two for her research, which makes forming friendships almost impossible. Two things saved me. Mother taught me to read when I was four. We were stranded in an airport for 18 hours on the way to a scientific conference in Italy where she was to give the keynote address. I took to it aggressively—reading I mean, not being stranded.

From then on, anytime I was forgotten at lessons, or if the sitter grew tired of waiting hours past Mother's expected arrival and left saying, "Your mom should be home any minute, sweetie, you'll be fine, I really must be going," always implying she didn't get paid enough to be treated like a non-person, I could spend my time reading. I could always escape into a cozy haven of fictional worlds. Unfortunately, the latter situation always caused Mother to have to restart the process of finding another sitter, a process that was exasperating and annoying for both of us.

I said two things saved me. The other was art. Those lessons I enjoyed immensely, partly because you could keep your artwork private if you didn't feel comfortable sharing, unlike dancing or gymnastics where everyone in the class could witness your gawky, embarrassing mistakes. Drawing was another escape. In these two pastimes, reading and art, I learned I could be alone without being lonely, so when we moved to Los Angeles right after my thirteenth birthday in January of this year, I told Mother not to schedule any more lessons because I was tired of feeling clumsy and talentless. I also insisted on absolutely no more sitters. School was only a block away, and I could take care of myself afterwards. I don't know who was more relieved, she or I.

The Salt Lake City airport was crowded. It was the end of May, and summer break had started yesterday, so families were headed out of town for their annual trips to the beach, or to see Grandma or whatever. I found my carousel at baggage claim without a problem, but Aunt Reverie didn't have a cell phone, so there was no way to call or text to let her know that I would be alone. Who doesn't have a cell phone now days anyway? Would she recognize me without Mother by my side? A familiar anxiety was beginning to twist in my gut, a feeling of being lost and alone. Would she be here? How would I know her?

"Lyric?" queried a voice right behind me. I spun on the balls of my feet to face a much younger, softer version of Mother. She had long black hair, casually caught up in a high ponytail, a creamy, rosy-cheeked complexion, and sparkling, startlingly bright blue eyes. I guessed she was in her mid-twenties. She was slim and pretty, dressed in jeans, a plain white t-shirt, and ratty flipflops.

"Yes," I breathed in a squeaky little voice filled with obvious relief. Not cool, so NOT COOL! Now, she would know how nervous I was.

"I'm Reverie Thindrell, or Aunt Reverie, I guess, but you can just call me Reverie. Where's your mother? Never mind, don't answer." She put her hand up in a stop gesture and laughed. Her laughter had the most beautifully melodious sound. Mother did not laugh near enough, and never with a carefree spirit like Reverie.

"If I know Mel, and I know my sister, then she is already off chasing the next new scientific discovery." She gave me a quick hug. She smelled like fresh meadows and sunshine, which was so different from the slightly chemical smell often accompanying Mother. Together we retrieved my two suitcases before rolling them to her black sport utility vehicle parked in the short-term parking garage.

"It will take a little more than an hour to get there, so you might as well get comfortable," she informed me after our seatbelts clicked and before settling into a companionable silence. As we traveled south, the landscape was dominated by a mountain range running parallel to the interstate on the left side of the car. The monstrous mountains seemed close enough to touch, although they were probably at least a mile or more away.

A huge valley stretched off to the right filled with thousands of houses and businesses, each suburb quickly merging into the next. There was another mountain range on the other side of the valley, but it looked small in comparison, probably because it was so far away and shrouded in commercial haze.

You might have been wondering why I wasn't going with Mother on her research trip, seeing as I had in the past, and why I was suddenly pawned off to an unknown relative. It all began after we moved to Los Angeles. I started having vivid dreams about flying. They were awesome. The weird thing was, when I woke up in the morning, my bedroom furniture would have moved in the night. I don't mean my bed was an inch closer to the wall; it would be halfway across the room, or my lamp would be out in the hallway. Once, we found my nightstand in the bathroom.

The super strange thing was, as if mysteriously moving furniture wasn't strange enough, a different piece of furniture moved each time, except for my framed poster of a famous asteroid cluster, which moved *every* time and was always found hanging slightly askew in a different room of the apartment. I briefly considered the fact that asteroids on a collision course hurtling through space might be a bad omen. It was like someone was trying to send me a message, "Warning: catastrophic events ahead." At first, I thought Mother was pulling a practical joke, but Mother isn't really a practical joker, and she assured me she was not responsible. Plus, she seemed genuinely worried. Let's face facts, I was genuinely worried!

Then the trouble started with Madison Roberts, a girl at school. First, there was the whispering and laughing behind my back just within earshot. Next, it was the name calling, and finally, a week before the last day of school; she tried to trip me in a crowded hallway. After an ugly moment of books dropping and arm flailing in ungraceful awkwardness, I managed to catch myself before I went sprawling. Several kids stopped, stared at me, and snickered. At first, I was embarrassed, but then I got angry. I whirled around and pointed my finger in her face, intending to yell at her, but before I could say anything, she literally flew backwards, smacking the floor on her rear end and sliding into a bank of lockers.

She insisted I had hit her, and all the witnesses corroborated her story, but I swear, I never even touched her. There are video cameras in the corridors, and after viewing the grainy footage I had to admit it looked like I had done *something* to her. Our school has a "zero tolerance policy" against violence, so I was suspended for the remainder of the term. Luckily, I had superior grades in all my classes, so I didn't fail seventh grade even though I wasn't allowed to take my finals.

At least Mother believed me, but she said it would be better if I went to Aunt Reverie's this summer instead of going with her to Japan. It felt like I was being punished for something I didn't do, and I'd been awfully bratty about it to her for the last week, but last night, I overheard her talking to my aunt on the phone. Reverie has a land line, even if she doesn't have a cell phone.

"You're the only person I'd trust with this issue. You've got to help her get this under control before she seriously hurts herself or, heaven forbid, someone else." A long pause and a sigh. "I know, I know, I just worry about her." Another pause, and Mother confirmed our flight arrangements and said thanks and goodbye and ended the call. The exchange made me realize perhaps Mother had a closer relationship with her sister than I had understood.

We exited the interstate in Orem, Utah, and headed east toward the mountain range. "See the Mountain there, the one with a little snow still on the very top?" asked Reverie as she pointed.

When I nodded, she continued, "That's Mount Timpanogos. It's the highest peak on the Wasatch Front. That's these mountains here." She gestured in a sweeping motion toward the range in front of us. "I live on the back side about halfway to the top. The Mountain is very special to our family."

"In what way?" I asked curiously. How could a mountain be special? Was she some kind of hiking enthusiast? *Please don't let it be hiking*, I thought.

Instead of answering my question, she asked one of her own, "There's some stuff we probably need to talk about before we get home. Your mom says strange things have been happening to you recently. Is that right?" Again, I just nodded. "What do you think is the explanations for those things?"

"Well," I took a deep shaky breath. "Mother has always taught me to use the scientific method when I have a problem to be solved. With the furniture, since Mother said it was not her, and I was the only other person in the apartment, it had to be me, so I thought I was doing it while I was sleepwalking. I looked it up online, and it's a real thing, and people do bizarre things with no memory of it after. And then..."

"And then?" she encouraged in a knowing tone, as if she knew sleepwalking was not the answer.

"Now, I'm not so sure, because this thing happened with Madison at school last week, and...and I was really mad at her...and I know I did NOT touch her, but I did something to her... I felt, oh, I don't know, some kind of energy flow out of me." I realized how stupid it sounded, so I added quietly, "I know, it's so lame."

"Energy, yes, a good word for it," she mused and then added, "But, you saw it on video, so you know it really happened, right? Did you consider that you might have special abilities?"

"What? Like superpowers?" I scoffed. The road divided, and we took the left fork onto the Provo Canyon Highway. It was a well-maintained four lane road with sweeping curves that climbed steadily in altitude. As we sped along the canyon floor, the mountain range pressed in close and soared above us on both sides of the car. I couldn't see the mountain tops without craning my neck. We passed a few houses, many more trees than in the valley, and even a couple of waterfalls that plunged down into the Provo River.

"You asked about Mount Timpanogos. My family has lived on the Mountain for generations. It gives us power, and we use that power for the good of those who live here. Your mother didn't inherit much of the ability to channel the power, sometimes that happens, but you seem to have gotten a double dose. I'm going to help you understand and control your abilities."

"What? I…" I licked my lips and looked nervously around the car for an escape. I was seriously beginning to wonder about the wisdom of Mother sending me to spend the summer with her deluded sister. As soon as Mother landed in Tokyo, I was going to call her and insist that she book me on the next flight to Japan.

Reverie must have sensed my distrust. Without taking her eyes off the road, she flicked her right wrist, causing a small yellow ball of transparent light to appear, it hovered above her open palm. We sped through a short tunnel, and the light grew brighter until we rushed out the other end. She snapped her fingers, and it disappeared just as we made the turn into a narrow side canyon.

Chapter 2

"It's called a witchlight. It comes in very handy when you forget your flashlight. I am a Witch, and so are you."

I hadn't gotten much sleep the night before because I'd been worried about this trip, and we'd had to get up extra early to drive to the airport in city traffic on a weekday morning. I rubbed my eyes wearily. Was I suddenly hallucinating as well as sleepwalking? And, did she just call me a witch?

I sullenly contemplated the scenery in disbelief. The road was now only two lanes, much steeper and more winding. We were climbing the back side of Mount Timpanogos. At first, the canyon was narrow, and there wasn't much to see but thick evergreens and a beautifully clear mountain stream that frothed and bubbled alongside the road as it came crashing down the mountain. Then the canyon opened and the view of Mount Timpanogos before us was breathtaking, dense green foliage at the base gave way to lightly snow-capped peaks, and the most pristine azure blue sky completely devoid of clouds above. There was such a sharp contrast between the snowy white peaks and the vast expanse of blue sky; it was other-worldly. Tiny glimpses of homes hidden among the trees dotted the lower slopes of the mountainside from small A-framed log cabins to gigantic lodges with banks of modern glass windows for enjoying the views.

"And Mother can't do that?" I asked abruptly.

"What? A witchlight? Yes, she can...or, at least, she could. It's one of the most basic spells, but the longer a Witch from our bloodline stays away from the Mountain and the farther she travels from it, the weaker her magic becomes. The fact that you have been manifesting power as far away as Los Angeles is really quite remarkable." She glanced at me and smiled reassuringly. I sat in stunned silence and shifted my gaze out the window again.

She pointed to the right, trying to orient me to my surroundings. "Fire station where we pick up our mail and take our trash." She gestured to the left. "Ski resort, called Riverwynd; there's not enough snow for skiing this time of year, but they have horseback riding, and mountain biking trails, and a zipline. The surrounding community is called Riverwynd, too." I think she was hoping that these activities might be appealing to me, but I wasn't very outdoorsy. I was more the geeky studious type.

After several steep switch backs, we took a side street off the main road. It was little more than a paved country lane with barely enough room for two cars going in opposite directions to pass one another, and that was optimistic depending on the size of the vehicles. The branches of the trees on the sides of the lane made a lovely canopy of green overhead as we traveled a hundred yards sharply downhill. At the bottom was a bridge over what I assumed was the same stream we had encountered on our way up the mountain. The bridge had large, round logs stripped of bark set at the four corners as posts and smaller tree branches as railings. On top of one of the posts sat an empty yellow mixing bowl. Reverie stopped the car, got out, and retrieved the bowl.

"It's better to just pay the tribute and not haggle with him," she remarked sheepishly as she stowed the mixing bowl in the back seat before continuing across the bridge and up another short incline. This just kept getting stranger and stranger.

"And here we are!" she proclaimed proudly as she pulled into a gravel driveway.

"Holy cliché, Batman!" I blurted in awe before I could think about how dumb that sounded.

The house resembled a storybook cottage I imagine Snow White might have inhabited. It was cream colored stucco with dark brown Tudor beam accents and trim, complete with a conical roofed turret, and faceted, leaded-glass windows. For an artist and reader like myself who had been raised in boring, white-box apartments, the house was a dream come true. I imagined all sorts of nooks and crannies and hidden passageways. It seemed to fit right into the densely wooded landscape, even though it wasn't a typical mountain cabin. There was only one house nearby, situated on a hill across the street. It was an impressive, sprawling modern lodge made of lacquered wood and cement. The lines of the architecture reminded me more of an art museum than a house.

"Who lives there?" I pointed in amazement.

"Our family friend and estate lawyer, Finnick Grey."

There were a few other houses barely visible farther down the lane, but they were almost completely obscured by aspens and maples and a few spruces that seemed predominate at this elevation. Reverie's house had a side entrance as well as one in the front.

"Let's go in the front door, so you can get your bearings," she remarked. Outside, the air smelled so cleanly fresh and woodsy. It was filled with the scent of damp earth and growing things, so different from this morning's smut and smog of Los Angeles.

We manhandled my bags up two curved stone steps onto the small flagstone front patio, and my aunt opened the unlocked arched oak door that was accented with old-fashioned wrought iron hinges and a small speak-easy window at peering height. We entered a foyer with wooden pegs on the left for hanging coats in the winter and a wooden bench below to sit and put on shoes. Several pairs of footwear were lined up neatly under the bench, and the bottom portion of an old butter churn was being used as an umbrella stand. There were ancient wide-plank hardwood floors studded with darker round wooden pegs throughout the entirety of the home.

"Welcome to Thimble Dell. It's a play on our last name, Thindrell. All the houses up here have names, like Fox Hollow, Deer Gully, and Hidden Glen. It's a quirky thing people do around here because street numbers are often hard to see and some of the streets don't even have names. Leave your luggage here, and I'll give you a quick tour. There are two floors above us and one below. I have some um...tenants who live in basement apartments." I filed this away as another curious thing to ask about later.

"This foyer is the hub of the house; all halls and stairways lead here." There was a staircase straight ahead that went up four steps and then made a 90-degree turn at a small landing before continuing up to what I assumed were the second and third stories. There was an arched doorway in front of us just to the left of the stair entrance showing a hallway which bisected the main floor. To my right and left in the foyer were identical archways leading to other parts of the house.

"So, if we go to the left here, this is the living room." The furnishings were cozy without being crowded and comfortable without looking shabby. It all had the old world style of a medieval English Tudor cottage, massive stone fireplace and hearth on the outer wall, nice, large, well-worn rug, and padded arm chairs and sofa in a mix of pretty patterns and solid fabrics to soften all the dark wood on the floors and the exposed beams on the ceiling, but no television or computer in sight. All the plaster walls in the house were painted a creamy color and studded here and there with the visible dark brown timber cross braces embedded in the stucco, as were commonly found in Tudor homes, some vertical, some horizontal, and even some diagonal.

"And through here," she indicated another open archway at the end of the room, "is the library." I inhaled sharply.

"Oh, it's wonderful," I exclaimed on the exhale. It was a perfect room with built in bookshelves covered in well-organized leather-bound books and a cushioned window seat with an array of fluffy pillows. There was a round table with two comfy chairs that could be used just as easily to play a game of checkers as it could to have a tea party on a rainy day, and the most incredibly snug looking buttery soft leather chair and footstool in the corner with an end table and lamp drawn up close enough for extra light to read by on a dark night, and a place to lay your open book if you needed to take a break to get a snack. French doors led to a covered deck that spanned the entire back of the house. When I stepped outside and peered over the railings, I noticed the flat part of the backyard could scarcely be more than 10 feet wide before dropping sharply downhill. You couldn't see the stream below because of all the trees, but you could hear the water rushing over the boulders. It was an oddly soothing sound.

As much as I would have liked to have stayed all day in the library, to be polite, I let Aunt Reverie usher me back the way we had come to the foyer.

"Now," she stated. "If we go to the right from here, we're in the dining room."

The dining area occupied the bottom floor of the turret, so it was a round room with a padded banquet seat built into the outer curve under the windows. In front of the bench was a round dining table with a couple of chairs drawn up to provide seating on the side of the table opposite the windows. A large, arched opening spilled into the surprisingly modern kitchen which contained granite countertops, stainless steel appliances, and a breakfast bar with stools. In the breakfast area was the side entrance to the house, which opened onto a covered wooden porch that would be handy for bringing in groceries during inclement weather.

When we retraced our steps to the foyer for the second time, we explored the hallway next to the staircase that connected both sides of the house. It contained a door under the stairs that went to the basement apartments, which we didn't open, and a door to the laundry room which we did.

"I have a...um, housekeeper, but I do my own laundry. There is a very particular rotating schedule for chores, and sometimes I'm in the mood to wear something that's dirty on a day not slated for laundry, so I just wash everything myself. It's easier and less complicated for me. I can do your laundry, too," she offered kindly.

"Oh, no, that's okay, I've been doing my own laundry for years now. I know what you mean about needing something that might be dirty and not wanting to wait until someone else has time to do laundry." At least Mother had figured out how to place an online grocery order to be delivered once a week and to have utility payments automatically deducted from her checking account. This after the electricity had been turned off twice because she had forgotten to pay the bill.

"I don't mind, and Mother would expect me to help. It's the least I can do," I assured her concerning the laundry. She was so thoughtful, and I couldn't risk offending her, at least not until I had some answers about this magic stuff, and I really didn't mind washing my clothes.

When the hall ended, it branched into a T-shape; straight ahead was a half bath, to the right was a back entrance to the kitchen, and to the left was an alternative way to access the library.

"Okay, I think, we've put it off long enough." She gave me the look of a fellow conspirator and winked, "Ready to haul those heavy cases up to the second floor?" Did she suspect the number of books I had hidden among my clothes?

I laughed and nodded. The carved millwork on the railings and banister, and the rich coffered wood paneling on the walls made the staircase itself an extraordinary work of art. The second story landing was open to the foyer below. There was a lovely geometrically patterned stained-glass window on this level situated high above the front door that spilled a rainbow of light onto the wooden foyer floor.

Again, we left the luggage while Reverie showed me the right side of the house where she had her complement of adjoining rooms containing her bedroom, bathroom, and her sitting room, which was located on the top story of the turret. The lofty inside of the conical roof with its exposed beams made for a very dramatic effect. When we trooped back to the landing, I noticed two other doors on this floor we had not yet explored, as well as the stairs going up to the third story.

"So, on this left side of the house are two additional bedrooms; one looks out onto the street and the other has a view of the woods. They are connected by a Jack and Jill bathroom. You can choose the bedroom you like most, or you can use both if you want. I mean, there's no one else up here but us, and since they're all connected it would be like having your own suite. One could be a bedroom and one could be your own private office or closet or whatever," she paused in her ramblings and swallowed. I got the impression that she was a little overly anxious to please me. I don't think anyone in my life had ever been overanxious to please me. I was used to either being overlooked completely or thought of as a nuisance.

"I know teenage girls like to have their space," she continued, "I'll leave you to look them over, and you can decide and unpack when you figure out what would be most comfortable for you. I'll be in my lab on the third floor with a late lunch when you get done. You can meet me there." She indicated the staircase behind her.

I thought it was nice of her to let me choose. I opened the first door and peered in. The front bedroom had a small Juliette balcony that faced the street and the house of the lawyer across from us. What was his name, Finn or something? The curtains, bedclothes, pillows, and an armchair were done in coordinating patterns of soft pink and cream; a bit too much pink for my taste, but still beautifully decorated. There was a queen-sized bed, bedside tables with matching lamps, a chest of drawers, and a wardrobe for hanging clothes, but no closet, plus a door into the shared bathroom.

I ventured through the bathroom into the back bedroom and fell in love the minute I opened the door. There was no balcony, but it had a sunny, built-in corner reading nook, perfect for cuddling up with a book. It contained furniture almost identical to the first bedroom but arranged with the bed against the inside wall shared with the bathroom rather than the outside wall like in the previous room. It was decorated in a toile fabric of Wedgewood blue on a background of cream. There were complimentary striped and floral fabrics in the same shade of blue scattered on the bed as well as in the soft furnishings of the nook and in the draperies. This bed, however, was a four-poster canopy bed with toile curtains that could be closed to make a hidden world.

In one corner there was a wrought iron banister and railings partially surrounding a round hole in the floor about 30 inches in diameter. On closer inspection I discovered it was the entrance to a metal spiral staircase, and upon descending the stairs I found myself once again in that wonderful library.

Chapter 3

I'd been so enthralled by all the books and comfy reading areas when I had been in the library earlier, I'd hardly noticed the twisting spiral staircase or even considered where it might ascend. Who needs a second bedroom when they can have cloistered access to a library full of books?

I was almost giddy with excitement when I ran, footsteps clanging, back up the spiral stairs. I opened my bedroom door and retrieved my belongings from the hallway. It didn't take long to empty the suitcases; underwear, socks, nightgowns, shorts, t-shirts, and jeans were all folded neatly into the chest of drawers. I arranged my shoes in a row on the bottom of the wardrobe and hung a few nicer blouses and skirts on the rack above. Then toiletries went into the drawers of the vanity in the bathroom, and my favorite books and a sketch pad with drawing pencils filled every drawer in both nightstands—all done. I decided to store my luggage in the empty wardrobe of the other bedroom.

I closed the bathroom door that went into the pink bedroom and thought dismissively, "*I probably won't go in there again until I have to pack to go back to Mother.*"

I bounced onto the queen-sized bed and surveyed my surroundings. This was a lovely room, much nicer than my room at home. In our apartment, my furniture consisted of a twin bed and a plain dresser. Mother tended to keep things minimalistic since we moved frequently, and she didn't have a lot of time for cleaning and straightening. While her methods were efficient, the apartment felt cold and austere.

I laid back and stared at the canopy above. I had to admit, I was excited about the prospect of superpowers. Maybe I could use them to get back at the girls who had been so nasty to me in school. It's not easy moving in the middle of the year, especially in junior high. Everybody has already formed their cliques and aren't interested in including the new girl, and those who had lived there the longest, like Madison Roberts, were the worst. Maybe I could just do magic on my own and be back with Mother in no time.

I thought about Reverie's witchlight and flicked my wrist trying to imitate her movement. Nothing happened. Frustrated, I tried again, and still nothing, not even a spark. My shoulders slumped, and I sighed. I hoped magic didn't require athletic ability because if it did, I was certainly doomed.

Dejectedly, I plugged my smart phone into the charger and realized not only was there no cell service here, but no Wi-Fi connection either. No wonder Reverie didn't have a cell phone! We were really in the middle of nowhere. It was okay, though. Mother knew the number to Reverie's landline, and there wasn't anyone else I needed to call. I was serious when I said I didn't have friends. There were a couple of nerdy girls, like myself, who had sat by me at lunch, but after my suspension, they had quickly dropped out of my life. My dearest friends had names like Bilbo Baggins, Harry Potter, and Anne (*of Green Gables*). I'd had some friends in other places where we had lived, and we had vowed to stay in touch when I'd relocated, but after a few emails back and forth, they'd moved on with their lives, and I was now out of sight, out of mind.

I didn't have social media accounts either. Mother said they weren't constructive for kids my age and thought my time might be better spent on my studies. Did I mention Mother is old-fashioned? Also, she reads a ton of medical journals that have strong opinions about the effects of social media on kids nowadays. My life would be so much easier if she wasn't such a freaking genius.

I would miss having internet access though. It was extremely helpful when you wanted to look up the meaning of a big word or get information fast, and I tended to want to do both. Regardless, my phone would keep the correct time. I glanced at it again, 2:00, that explained my ferocious hunger. I hadn't had anything to eat since a rushed breakfast in the Los Angeles airport, so I set off to find the third floor.

This staircase was enclosed, and the wooden treads and risers were a bit steeper and narrower than the main stairs. As I climbed, my head popped up above the attic floor before the rest of my body made its way to the top, so I could see the room before I had fully arrived. While the walls and ceilings were insulated and plastered, the thick, heavy oak rafters and beams were exposed and, because the room was located right up under the irregularly shaped gables of the steeply pitched roof, it contained an array of nooks and crannies and half walls that met with low, sharply sloped ceilings.

You might think it would be a dark space, but there were French doors to a small deck off the back and a place to one side where the ceiling had been bumped up for extra height, which formed a little sitting alcove containing two overstuffed arm chairs and windows that looked out over the side yard. There was a wood burning stove, cold now, sitting on a hearth of brick with the same brick on the wall behind. There was also a small, old-fashioned curve-top refrigerator in a shade of turquoise and a farmhouse sink. Lining the other walls were an array of cupboards, cubby holes, shelves, and cabinets all containing neatly labeled jars, books, papers, old-fashioned scales and an odd assortment of other things. There was even a small half bath through a door tucked out of sight under one of the eaves.

In the middle of the room was a large, long, high table with a stainless-steel top and big, beefy wooden legs and iron cross braces. This space had the same rich hardwood floors as the rest of the house, but there were no plush area rugs under foot. A couple of padded stools with high backs were drawn up to the table, and Reverie was seated on one of them, unconsciously swiveling side to side taking notes. She glanced up as I appeared and pushed a lock of dark hair that had escaped her ponytail behind her ears. She had haphazardly kicked off her cheap rubber flip-flips under the table.

"Well?" she asked excitedly as her blue eyes sparkled, "Which room did you chose?"

"The blue one."

"Oh, I'm so glad," she beamed as she performed a rapid, enthusiastic, and noiseless clapping gesture with the palms of her pretty hands. "That was my room growing up. If you open the windows, you can hear the brook at night, and of course, there is the library too. I knew you would love that. Mel said you liked to read."

I found it odd that she referred to Mother in such a familiar way. Few people called her by her first name, Demelza, much less a nickname. Her colleagues, my teachers, and even our landlord knew she preferred to be called Dr. Thindrell.

She smiled warmly.

"Come, and have a sandwich. We won't usually eat lunch this late, so this is just a snack to tide you over. Don't eat too much. Dinner is at 6:00, and I want you to meet Allegra, one of my boarders."

"How long have you lived here?" I asked curiously as I picked up half of a ham sandwich and hungrily began to munch. It had a tangy sauce I didn't recognize and was surprisingly good for a ham sandwich.

"Your mother and I were born in this house. The pink bedroom was hers. My mother, your grandmother, was born here as well. Her name was Elowen Noble Thindrell. My grandmother and grandfather built this house in the 1940s, right after they were married. A few years ago, I modernized the kitchen, laundry room, and baths, and added some apartments in the basement. I tried to keep some of the original charm by not adding a bunch of walk-in closets and stuff. They didn't have those back when the house was built."

"What were their names—my great grandparents?" I asked. Mother never talked about her relatives. We didn't have any pictures of them either. I desperately wanted to belong to somebody or something. It was hard to form connections to people when you moved as much as we did. It was better to stay aloof; then it didn't hurt so much when you had to leave.

"He is Alaric James Noble, Ric for short; and she was Lorelei Killian, or Lorelei Noble after they married. She was a great Witch, and he, a really accomplished Warlock. Their parents and most of their friends were killed in a battle against a wicked Warlock named Jasper Finch soon after they were married. They inherited a lot of land and property around here after the battle."

"What happened to the Warlock, Jasper?" I liked it here and wasn't comfortable with the thought of a wicked Warlock lurking about, whatever a Warlock was.

"Together, they defeated and killed him."

I wasn't sure if I found that shocking or reassuring. I glanced at her notes.

"What is it exactly that you do?" I inquired cautiously. I hoped there wouldn't be toad eyes, or bat guano involved in this magic junk. Eww!

"Well, that's complicated. I make quite a nice income by renting out all my grandparent's properties to vacationers. This is a popular destination for the rich and famous. They come here in the winter to ski and to hike and mountain bike in the summer. I am also a sort of doctor to the nonhuman population that inhabit the Mountain."

"What exactly do you mean by nonhuman?" I asked with narrowed eyes. "You mean animals? Are you like a veterinarian?" She sighed.

"I guess it's time we had our first lesson in witchcraft. Lyric, you and I are not human. A Witch's DNA is slightly different from a human. We can mate with humans, but we can only produce offspring with another one of our kind." Something about that statement was important, but I needed to think about it later; right now, all I could focus on was the nonhuman aspect of the conversation.

"Witch is a generic term that includes both female Witches and male Warlocks," she continued as she took a sandwich for herself with her long slim fingers. I noticed her fingernails lacked polish, but were clean, short, and neatly filed.

"So, there are other Witches here that you give check-ups to and such?" I asked with a puzzled frown.

"No," she said with a tiny smile, "remember that great battle that I told you about? All the other viable Witches around here were either killed then or have gone since. You and I are the only ones left here, and besides, Witches don't need check-ups anyway. We don't catch human diseases. We aren't immortal, but we live extraordinarily long lives, and we age much slower than humans." That probably explained why I had perfect attendance at school, and why Mother never believed me when I said I needed to stay home because I didn't feel well.

"Then who is it that you treat?" I asked suspiciously. I wanted to know partly because last Saturday I had spent a rare day with Mother in her research lab. I think I was there mainly because she didn't completely trust me to be home alone, especially after the incident with Madison at school the day before. At the lab, Mother had received a biomedical package containing blood samples. I happened to get a good look at the shipping label, because she seemed unusually pleased with this delivery, but until this second, I hadn't connected the fact that the package had been sent from Reverie's address.

"Only a couple dozen of the 200 houses at Riverwynd are inhabited all year; the rest are rental properties or summer homes for wealthy humans. Most of the people who live here fulltime are other species of magical creatures, called Fae. Some inhabit manmade structures, but others don't. They can't catch human diseases either, but sometimes, they get injured, or need help with childbirth, or want a potion made or a talisman crafted. That's my job. Actually, it's more than my profession; it's my family's legacy, my calling, or life's work. As long as one of our female line is here to help the inhabitants of the Mountain, we are promised certain personal powers and physical blessings, and the ecological balance of the Mountain is maintained."

"So, you want me to live here and learn from you and eventually take over your responsibilities?" I asked with wide eyes. Don't get me wrong, Reverie was nice, she didn't treat me like a little kid, and it seemed like she would be a patient teacher, but I was scared. What if I wasn't good at magic? So far, my so-called magical abilities had caused me nothing but trouble. I was afraid of failure, and I didn't want to let my aunt down.

I liked school. Well, I liked learning, and I made good grades. I didn't really care for the social aspects of school, but I was good at remembering things and taking tests. I hated group projects because I preferred to work alone, and I could guarantee the outcome if I didn't have to rely on partners. I was dreadful at team sports or anything requiring hand-eye coordination and was always the last person picked for any team. Since kindergarten, I had been the shortest person in my class, and I was terribly skinny.

The lessons Mother had arranged for me often included public performances, and I really hated those. I have terrible stage fright. I spent the summer Mother enrolled me in drama lessons painting stage scenery in a backroom by myself while everyone else was on stage rehearsing. The director of the play was so grateful, she probably didn't notice when I didn't show up for the actual show. At afterschool choir, I volunteered to alphabetize the conductor's vast collection of sheet music during rehearsals to avoid having to sing in public. After he heard my tuneless voice, he was quick to take me up on my offer, which meant Mother paid him for me to work. It was a satisfactory arrangement for all of us. Mostly, I conveniently forgot to inform Mother about the class recitals, so then I didn't have to participate.

"You don't have to decide anything right now," she assured kindly. "We will probably live for hundreds of years, and I may have a daughter of my own someday. I would like to train you to use your powers safely, and pass on my knowledge to you, so you can make an informed decision." Living for hundreds of years was a dizzying prospect in and of itself.

"And what happens if we both leave for good?" I asked this more to gather information than anything else. I know I had only been here for a couple of hours, but already I felt a special kinship towards this place. It was peaceful, and for some reason, I felt at home for the first time in my life.

"Once, almost 60 years ago, the Caretaker of the Mountain was lost, forcibly taken away. She didn't find her way home for 18 years, and during that time, she almost lost her mind. The magical population here significantly declined, and the Mountain suffered years of serious drought and a deadly wildfire."

"Okaaay." I forced myself to stop staring at her and swallowed a mouthful of dry sandwich. "So...not a responsibility to be taken lightly? I think I need to know more about magical creatures. What are we talking about? Hobbits? Elves?"

"No such thing as hobbits," she laughed that merry laugh again. "They were a figment of Tolkien's imagination. Elves? Hmmm...depends on your definition. They prefer to be called Brownies and are more like Santa's elves, or the fable, *The Shoemaker and the Elves*, or J.K. Rowling's house elves than a character such as Legolas." She chuckled at the disappointment on my face. Well, come on, Legolas was cute; Dobby was not.

"What else?" I asked curiously.

"Pixies, Fauns, Centaurs, Naiads, Dryads, Dwarfs, and Elementals."

"Fairies?" I asked hopefully.

"I suppose you mean those small winged creatures?" she questioned. "No, too cold here for those in the winter, but we have Pixies. They're a hardier race." Her answer did not rule out the existence of what I knew as Fairies.

"The term 'Faerie' is actually a general term for all the people of the Fae races. With a few exceptions, the Fae come from Faerie Kingdoms in a parallel world known as the Everafter. They are usually immortal but will die if they receive a wound severe enough."

"Any others I should know about?" I scrunched up my brows and narrowed my eyes trying to rapidly compartmentalize all this new information before my brain exploded.

"Yes, we have a Bridge Troll named Clyde, and one of my boarders is a Kitsune, but there are others who don't like making contact with the outside world." I supposed she had offered some sort of tribute to the Bridge Troll on her way to the airport for him to let her cross his bridge unharmed, and that's why she had collected the empty mixing bowl on the way home. Oh, come on, I had read *Three Billy Goats Gruff*. What kid hasn't?

"What's a Kitsune?" I asked curiously. This was something I had never some across in any fantasy literature.

"A shapeshifter who has a human form and a fox form, originally

27

from Japan. I'm not as familiar with Japanese mythology as I am with our own European ancestors, and Allegra is reticent to share, but I know she has other magical abilities besides shapeshifting. She teaches pottery and sells local artist's paintings and hand-made soap to vacationers at *The Art Hut* down at Riverwynd Ski Resort."

"And her name is Allegra, like the allergy medicine?" I asked in disbelief.

"Yes," chortled Reverie, "exactly like that. The Fae tend to have unusual names. Most of our nonhuman population around here work for the resort."

"How do they get away with that? Don't people freak out if they see a nonhuman?" I was no expert, but I had seen enough horror movies to know people weren't afraid to use violence if they felt threatened by something otherworldly.

"To non-magical eyes they appear human. They can create a certain magical illusion or glamour." She paused, "I mean, well, Pixies appear as dragonflies and Dwarfs are just little people to most humans. Allegra, my boarder, seems like an Asian woman with red hair to non-magical persons. Centaurs and the rest create a glamour that makes them appear human to everyone else, but as a Witch, you should be able to see their true selves."

"What about Brownies?"

"Friendly little things, without exception," she said affectionately. "Brownies can be invisible if they want, so they're rarely ever seen by humans. Best housekeepers around. They love to clean; no, they live to clean! Several families work for me to tidy up my properties after every vacationer goes home." A sudden horrifying idea struck her. "Don't get any 'Hermione Granger Frees the House Elves' ideas either. Never, ever offer them clothes. It offends them greatly, and they will leave and never return if they get insulted. They are very proud and steeped in the old-world customs. I buy them a bolt of linen every year, and they make their own clothing, but it can only be linen and nothing else, and I can't offer it to them directly. I have to 'lose' it somewhere in the woods for them to find." She made air quotes around the word lose when she spoke.

"How are they able to clean human houses, aren't they tiny?" I was genuinely curious.

"About two feet tall. They can lift 100 times their own weight and can levitate and teleport from one place to another. Really remarkable creatures. You can't pay them, but you can offer shelter, and they take whatever food they need from your pantry. I have one living here, you know?"

"Really?" Though I trusted she was telling the truth, I was still having trouble shifting my paradigm to include a universe where mythological creatures were real.

"He's been with my family for over nine decades. His name is Ezekiel, but we've always called him Zeke."

"What's he like?" I put my sandwich down. The bread had started to dry out, and I was no longer hungry anyway. The conversation was more interesting than food.

She hesitated for a moment to think of an accurate description.

"Joyous, playful, fiercely loyal, helps me not to take life too seriously..." She paused and glanced at me. I'm sure my expression belayed my confusion. "Oh, you mean what does he *look* like? Well, he has very brown skin, hence the name Brownies."

"Did you just use hence in a sentence?" I asked jokingly.

"Give me a break," she countered good-naturedly. "I read a lot of archaic books. Overall, Brownies are dark skinned and incredibly wrinkled, like shriveled apples, no matter their age. They have a mop of thick brown hair that tends to stick up every which way, pointy ears, and green eyes—extremely clear, intelligent green eyes. Their hands, feet and head are disproportionately large for their body size, and they don't ever wear socks or shoes, even in the dead of winter."

"Hey, speaking of books," she interrupted herself. I looked at her quizzically. Um, were we speaking of books? "Since we have time before dinner, I have a book about the characteristics of magical creatures. It's probably well below your reading level, but extremely informative, especially for a novice. Would you like to look at it?" Then she gave me the most beguilingly innocent look with those big baby blue eyes.

Now you know the story of how I came to be doing homework on the first day of summer vacation.

Chapter 4

Magical Creatures and How to Know Them was extremely interesting, even if the language was rather simple, and it had obviously been written as a textbook for primary school Witches, but I was a sucker for a good book, and obviously Reverie was already learning how to exploit this information. It included a plethora of colorful illustrations and some enlightening facts. Among other things, I learned Bridge Trolls are ugly but harmless, and Fauns (not to be confused with fawns) have the upper body of a man and the lower body of a goat, but only have two legs, while Centaurs have the upper body of a man and the lower body of a horse, yet they have four legs. I got so caught up in reading, I was surprised when I heard a series of chimes. The doorbell? A phone?

"Dinner's ready. We'd better hurry. Zeke will be unhappy if we let his cooking get cold, and I don't want to keep Allegra waiting." As we tripped merrily down the steps, Reverie remarked. "Allegra usually has to work until 7:00 during the summer months, but she got Briar to cover her shift tonight because she wanted to meet you."

I think the implication was for me to mind my manners. When we arrived in the dining room, we found the Kitsune already seated, and the food on the table.

"Allegra, I would like you to meet my niece, Lyric Thindrell."

Allegra had almond shaped eyes with irises the color of melted dark chocolate. Her hair was loose, hung below her waist, and was a rusty auburn color with two streaks of platinum, one on each side of her face. She had the soft, smooth, slightly olive-tinted skin of a young adult, but her bearing and her clothing spoke of a woman much older. She sat ramrod straight, her hands folded demurely in her lap, and wore a floor-length, high-necked, long-sleeved Victorian gown in a shade of midnight blue, which had probably been the height of fashion in the early twentieth century. I was super glad Mother had insisted I wear nice pants and a button down, collared shirt for travel.

"Lyric, this is my boarder Allegra Watanabe."

"It's a pleasure to meet you, Ms. Watanabe," I said as I stepped forward and extended my hand. As an only child of a single parent, I spent most of my time in the company of adults and had been well schooled in proper etiquette. She took my hand, and I gave her a firm handshake. From the pleased gleam in her eyes, I could immediately sense I had passed a test.

"Please, call me Allegra. Come now, sit, everyone. There's fried chicken tonight, and I'm famished." The irony of a fox-woman eating chicken was not lost on me. My stomach growled in solidarity, the discarded half sandwich and measly LAX yogurt parfait were long gone. There was indeed fried chicken, and it was excellent fried chicken, but there were also mashed potatoes with gravy, biscuits, corn on the cob, coleslaw, and later, I found there was homemade apple pie with ice cream for dessert.

The table had been set with the best china and silver. Each plate was accompanied by a starched white linen dinner napkin with petite blue flowers delicately embroidered across one end. In order to promote comfortable dinner conversation, I took a chair with my back to the kitchen, so I could face Reverie and Allegra who sat on the padded bench. At first, we busied ourselves with filling our stomachs, and our limited discussion had a stilted uncomfortable quality that sometimes accompanies the attempts at small talk by an introvert. Although, to her credit, Allegra did try by asking a few polite questions about my travel. From Reverie's revelations, I discovered there wasn't this abundance of food and fancy dinnerware for every meal, but my arrival was considered a special occasion, and so Zeke had unleashed this culinary feast.

"Lyric is an artist from what I hear," Reverie stated. She absolutely had a closer relationship with Mother than I had realized. Allegra perked up immediately. I could tell we had hit upon her passion.

"Oh, my dear, I would love to see some of your work." Her eyes sparkled for the first time.

"Well, I'm just a beginner. I do mostly pencil sketches right now, but I'm always interested to learn from other artists. Aunt Reverie tells me you're a potter." When uncomfortable with attention and praise, always turn the conversation back to the person shining the spotlight on you. It works every time.

"I teach pottery classes from May to November, and then the skiers take over the Mountain. In the winter months, I sit behind the cash register and sell the occasional painting or read a book. You should walk down to *The Art Hut* and join one of my classes sometime. The gallery is tiny, but we display paintings and other works by local artists, and there is a large display window into the soap maker's workshop. Her name is Briar Faye, and she crafts on Mondays and Thursdays." She lowered her voice, something I've noticed women do when speaking disparagingly of others, and added as a whispered gossipy aside, "To get a Dryad to commit to even that much work is astounding, but she seems to fancy what she does."

"I would love to visit you if Aunt Reverie will let me out of class." I was sincere. Art, in all forms gave me great pleasure. With art, a person could make an important statement without having to say anything out loud or participate in a nerve-wracking public performance. It made me feel like I could be heard when no one else was listening to me, and I enjoyed contemplating what other artists had to say.

"All work and no play makes Jill a dull girl, or something similar," she joked and then continued, "There is also an outdoor glass blowing studio adjacent to *The Art Hut*, and the Tram family, some local people, blow glass there until November. It's so fascinating to watch, almost like a well-choreographed dance. The resort has two restaurants, plus a deli and a bar, and they recycle all their broken dishes, alcoholic beverage bottles, and empty glass jars. The Trams melt it down and use this recycled glass exclusively in creating new blown glass. I've been told that using recycled glass for blowing glass has unique challenges. They make things like drinking glasses, vases, serving vessels, Christmas ornaments, and other sculptural pieces that we sell in the shop.

"Reverie," she insisted plaintively, "You really must allow the girl some time off from learning Witchcraft. Why, an education without art is no education at all!"

At this outburst, I noticed her nose started to take on a decidedly elongated foxy appearance, and fur tufted ears sprouted from the top of her head. I tried terribly hard not to stare.

"Allegra," Reverie chuckled, "I have no intention of driving her like a slave master. She'll have plenty of free time for pursuing the arts."

The Kitsune's face melted into her human form as she visibly relaxed.

Allegra and I talked at length about art museums we had both visited, including the Louvre in Paris, The Met in New York City, Belvedere Palace in Vienna, and some of the great works of art housed in each place, Di Vinci's *Mona Lisa*, Jackson Pollock's *Autumn Rhythm (Number 30)*, and Gustave Klimt's *The Kiss*. While we chatted merrily, Reverie eventually started to clear the table. I made a move to help, but she shook her head and nodded toward Allegra. I understood it was my task to entertain our guest. From my position at the table, I couldn't see into the kitchen, but I heard her have a soft conversation with someone, probably Zeke, the house Brownie, before she returned with the filled dessert dishes on a tray. Much later, she left again, taking the empty dessert plates and returning with a choice of herbal tea or hot cocoa.

After what seemed like hours of food and conversation, shadows were starting to lengthen outside the dining room windows. Nighttime comes late this time of year, but I could tell the sun was already sinking, telling me darkness gathered earlier here once the sun descended behind the mountains. I'm sure the fatigue of the day combined with my sleepless night was showing on my face when Reverie gently suggested that I might want to go up and spend some time unwinding alone in my room before retiring for the night. I appreciated her diplomacy in letting me have control of the situation without telling me it was bedtime like I was a child. I felt very mature. I hadn't realized how tired I was until I was given an excuse to leave. I said thank you and goodnight, and made my way upstairs.

During the time my room had been unoccupied, someone had turned down my bed covers, opened the windows, turned on my bedside lamp, and placed the book I left in the attic, *Magical Creatures and How to Know Them,* on my nightstand. The breeze from the open windows felt fresh and cool and carried the scent of evergreens. I could hear the gurgling sounds of the stream rushing along at the bottom of the hill. It was a comforting and peaceful sound, and it made me feel welcomed.

"Thank you, Zeke," I called softly into the shadows, but only silence answered.

In the bathroom, I unwrapped the new bar of soap with a printed label that read *Briar Faye's Handmade Soap-Rosemary Mint.* I took a long, hot shower and found the soap fantastically refreshing. I wondered idly if Briar made other varieties of soap besides rosemary mint. Afterward, I quickly toweled dry, and as I brushed my teeth, I gazed into the mirror; blue eyes in the same color as Mother and Reverie's stared back at me. I had medium brown, non-descript, shoulder length hair. It was fine and straight, and I parted it on the side, so it fell over my right eye on occasion, which I hoped made me look mysterious. It wasn't all that effective because I had a sprinkling of freckles across my cheeks and nose, which everyone said were so cute—just my luck—too cute to be mysterious. I was short for my age and thin with no real curves yet.

I slipped on my nightgown and crawled into bed. I had planned to read up on Dryads but found I was just too exhausted. It wasn't late, and I thought I would have trouble falling asleep, but it had been a long day full of crazy revelations. In reflection, I could rationalize that all I had actually seen with my own eyes was an aunt who could do a magic trick with a glowing light and a lady whose features, in the fading light of day, sometimes resembled a fox. On the other hand, the fact that magic was real was far less confusing to me than the explanation that I had suddenly become a closet sleepwalker who moved furniture in the night or shoved people without any memory of the act.

I tried to push it all out of my mind. I could think about it more clearly tomorrow. The profound quiet of the mountains and the distant sound of rushing water was so relaxing; before I knew it, I was drifting off to sleep.

In my dream, I heard a frustrated male voice whispering under my bed.

"I just want to *see* her. To reassure myself that she is alright."

"And I am under strict orders from Miss Reverie that she does not *see* you, Doc...for now," said a different male voice. Little men under the bed, what a silly dream. I must be much more distraught and exhausted than I thought.

Chapter 5

When I woke, it was still dark outside. I glanced at my phone to see it had just turned 5:00 in the morning. Ugh, way too early to be awake in the summertime. I rolled over and tried to resume sleep, but it evaded me. Maybe going to sleep before 9:00 had been a bad idea, or maybe it was just the new environment. I got up, threw on some shorts and my favorite t-shirt, and hastily brushed my hair and teeth, then crept barefoot down the spiral staircase to browse the library shelves for something interesting to read.

The lights in the back hallway and kitchen were on, and I heard Reverie and several male voices coming from the kitchen. Thinking I might be able to finally meet Zeke, the Brownie, I poked my head around the corner and stopped dead in my tracks when I saw Reverie sitting on a stool at the end of the breakfast bar in deep conversation with three…mice? No, not mice; maybe they were hamsters, sitting on their haunches on the countertop. When I say "in conversation," I mean they were talking back to her.

"Hello?" I called cautiously, "What's all this?"

Reverie's head popped up and all three of the not-mice turned towards me simultaneously.

"Well, that decides it," said one of the not-mice, "Cat's out of the bag now!"

Their voices were not high-pitched and squeaky as you might imagine, but rich and deep like any average male voice would be. Their fur was a mix of sandy blonde and cinnamon brown with accents of charcoal gray. Each one had a different and distinctive fur pattern.

They were kind of cute with their long twitchy whiskers, a fact I was not quite willing to admit just yet.

"That's a terrible analogy," protested a second not-mouse. "Cats, I hate cats!" He visibly shuddered. They were very expressive for such tiny beady-eyed creatures.

"Lyric," uttered Reverie guiltily. First, she sighed, then obviously making up her mind about something, she sat up straighter and squared her shoulders as if she had come to an important decision. "You might as well come in and have a seat."

I perched tentatively on the edge of a bar stool.

"Your mom and I thought it might be best to wait to give you time to adjust to all of the changes before I gave you any more shocking news," she hesitated then took a deep breath to reassure herself, "Lyric, may I introduce you to my grandfather Alaric Noble, my father…who would be your grandfather…Westley Thindrell, and your father, Dr. Vinn Everton." The not-mice each bowed in turn. Well, wasn't this just craptastic!

"What?" I screeched in disbelief, "How is it possible my father is a mouse?" I knew my voice was too loud and close to hysteria, but I couldn't seem to help myself.

"We are not mice," protested my great-grandfather, Alaric, with dignity. "We are American pikas. Mice are classified under the order of Rodentia, but we are lagomorphs, more akin to a rabbit than a nasty mouse." He sniffed and seemed greatly offended by my outburst.

Reverie rolled her eyes and cast him a disparaging glance as if to say his information was not helpful in this situation.

"But," he sputtered defensively, "We have fur, not hair like mice."

"Mice are nocturnal, and pikas are diurnal," added my not-mouse father, Vinn, quietly, almost self-consciously. Was he trying to help? He was definitely not helping.

38

I simply refused to believe this was happening, it had gone on long enough. I pointed at the little grouping of furry bodies, "Somebody better tell me what is going on!"

No one dared to speak. They all looked at each other nervously. I shot daggers at Reverie with my eyes as I tried to hold back tears.

"I want to talk to Mother, right now!" I demanded.

"Aw, honey, your mom probably just got to her hotel after a 15-hour flight. Its 11:00 at night in Tokyo. Just let us explain, and if you still want to call her, we'll call."

I angrily blinked back tears and nodded uncertainly.

Reverie sighed again. "This may take a while. I'll make us some breakfast. Ric, you'd better go first. Start at the beginning," she warned as she slipped off the bar stool. Ric was the pika with the lightest bits of fur in his coloring.

Alaric Noble, my great-grandfather, also known as Ric, cleared his throat and began to speak.

"I grew up on the Mountain with a boy named Jasper Finch. We had the misfortune of both falling in love with the same girl; her name was Lorelei Killian." He paused and smiled, staring off into space until one of the other pikas gently nudged him. He came to himself and continued, "Jasper didn't start out as a bad sort, but his mother died when he was young, and his father turned to the black arts, necromancy, Demon worship, blood rituals and the like. The father abused the boy, physically and mentally, until he became a twisted mess. We found out later that Jasper had murdered his father and kept it secret for many years, claiming the father had abandoned him. Lorelei said he was tender when he courted her, although sometimes she saw a violent, possessive side, and it made her nervous. When he found I was wooing her too, he gave her an ultimatum: choose him or else.

"She didn't take him seriously. We were young and in love. We didn't realize just how powerful he had become, or how much of his father's taste for black magic he had inherited until it was too late. Lorelei chose me, and we were married. In the ceremony during the part where the officiator says, 'If anyone objects to this union let him speak now, or forever hold his peace,' Jasper appeared in the back of the chapel and spoke these words:

The moment you receive your heart's desire,
A pint-sized beast I create of the sire.
Not just you, but all of your line,
Forever more 'til the end of time."

"His poetry stinks by the way," interjected my grandfather, Westley Thindrell, whose coloring included the greatest number of darker patches. I gave him an annoyed glance.

"No comments from the peanut gallery," chimed Reverie from the pantry. "You'll get your chance, Dad."

"I don't really understand." I remarked in confusion.

"I think it will all become clear, little Ricky," said Ric. I scowled. I guess Rick or Ricky could be a nickname for Lyric, but I did not want to share a name with this little creature, and I certainly was not ready for diminutive terms of endearment from the not-mouse.

"What happened next?" I inquired, ignoring his comment. Okay, so sue me; I was intrigued by the story.

Ric shrugged.

"He made a grand exit and we continued with the ceremony. During the next few months, it became more and more apparent to us that he was a bad egg, sadistic and bloodthirsty. The Witches in the area took sides either for him or against him." Then he called to

Reverie in an aside, "Did you tell her we say Witches when we mean female Witches and male Warlocks?"

"Yes," she spoke over her shoulder as she assembled ingredients.

"In the end," Ric continued, "There was a great battle and many lives were lost, but together Lorelei and I defeated Jasper. We supposed the Curse had ended with his death, because that's customarily what happens. We weren't even sure there had been a Curse because we had not seen any evidence of it yet.

"Witches live long lives and age extremely slowly. We built this house and tried for many years to have a child. Normally, Witches can only have one child in our lifetimes, and infertility abounds, so babies are precious. Finally, 15 years after our wedding, Lorelei became pregnant, but the morning after conception...as far as we can tell...I woke up in this form. I had no magic. I could speak, although only magical creatures could understand me. If I ever tried to leave the Mountain, I got only as far as the mouth of Provo Canyon, and I would disappear and reappear in this house."

Ric sat on his haunches on the breakfast bar, and as he spoke, he gestured excitedly with his little paws to add emphasis to his story. I kept making covert glances at my father, but he was paying rapt attention to Ric's story as if he had never heard it before, which I found highly suspicious. I got the feeling he was rather nervous about meeting me and was avoiding eye contact on purpose.

"Lorelei asked our neighbor, Mr. Finnick Grey, an attorney, to set up a trust for our child in case anything happened to us. She was obsessive about securing the baby's future. We didn't know if I would live a normal Witch's lifespan, or the shorter three to four years of an average pika. The trust included all the property we had inherited after the great battle, our current home, and our other assets. Finnick was the executor. The rental properties generated quite a healthy income.

"Of course, she was devastated by my transformation, but she always had faith she could crack Jasper's spell. I couldn't help her except in an advisory capacity because, as I stated, I no longer had any magic, and I was trying to learn how to adapt to the limitations of my new body. When we first defeated Jasper, she often fell into bouts of melancholy because she felt guilty about his death, saying maybe we hadn't done enough to save him. After I was enchanted, she was determined to find Jasper's grimoire and undo the Curse."

"Hold on a minute," I interrupted. "Grimoire?"

I was trying super hard to keep up, but as you might expect I was feeling more than a tad overwhelmed. I was immersing myself into a new language and culture, but instead of gently dipping my foot into the pool to test the waters, I felt as if someone was blasting me with a firehose.

"It's like a personal journal all Witches keep to document their rituals, and any magic recipes they have perfected, as well as some notes on how successful their spells were as they tweaked them, and maybe even some personal goals with thoughts and opinions thrown in as well," Reverie reported as she whipped up a batter. She made the grimoire sound like a cross between a preteen's diary and a family cookbook.

"It took her months to find it hidden in his old house," continued Ric. "She spent hours in our attic sanctuary trying to break the spell he had placed on the grimoire which allowed only the true owner to read the contents. After several more months, she was finally able to break the spell and start to decipher the book. Three weeks before our child was due, she told me she had made a significant breakthrough, but she didn't want to get my hopes up before she knew if her hypothesis was correct.

"Unfortunately, the next day, she went into premature labor. At first, she told me she had eaten something that didn't agree with her; maybe she was in denial about the baby coming ahead of schedule, or maybe she just didn't want to alarm me, but that afternoon, she finally phoned the doctor she had been seeing in the valley, and two human midwives drove up to assist her. One was an older more experienced nurse, and the other was a young novice. It was not a long or difficult labor. The baby was born about midnight, a girl, but that was no surprise, because the Mountain *always* provides a female heir.

"She was exhausted, but she dictated the information for the birth certificate to the young midwife while the older one was giving the baby an examination. We had picked out the name Elowen Alexandra Noble. Lorelei told the nurse I was deceased, and because they saw our wedding photos proudly displayed, they had no cause to doubt, so that information went on the certificate.

"I had to watch from a hiding place. Humans don't take kindly to small furry beasts, especially around newborns. When the older midwife was occupied with something, I crept down and took a closer look at my beautiful child. The nurse had given her a pacifier, which Elowen promptly spit out. Lorelei was diametrically opposed to the things, so I snatched it away and hid it. One minute, Lorelei was there, smiling weakly and so proud, and the next moment, she turned blue and passed out. The room was suddenly full of panic."

"What happened?" I whispered weakly as Reverie set a plate of pancakes in front of me.

"She passed away," he said sadly. After all these years, I could tell it still pained him to say it. "They called the coroner, and he took her body away before the night was over. Then, they packed all our perishable food, carted it out to their car because they didn't want it to spoil in an empty house, and whisked my 'orphaned' baby away."

I sat in stunned silence staring at my pancakes. I had let myself get completely sucked into the story.

"Eat," said Reverie, the nurturer. "It will make you feel better." I took my knife and fork and began to cut the cakes into itty bitty triangles. It was something methodical to do while my mind raced.

"But you got her back, right? The baby, Elowen?" Somewhere in the back of my mind I remembered Reverie saying, "*The Caretaker of the Mountain was lost, forcibly taken away.*"

"The lawyer, Finnick, was out of the country on business. I had no way of reaching him. I couldn't use a telephone because of my size, we had only rotary dial in those days, and humans couldn't understand me when I spoke anyway. Lorelei had sent Zeke, our Brownie, to stay with nearby kin, while she was in labor. She thought it would be hard for him with humans tripping about the house all hours of the day and night.

"When Zeke returned the next day, he was able to place a call to Finnick's offices in town, and his human secretary got a message to him in London. He returned two days later and discovered Lorelei had been buried in a pauper's field in Provo. Having power of attorney for our estate, he was able to get her grave moved up here, but he couldn't find Elowen. It took us three years to find out the young midwife had written our surname as Mobile on the birth certificate instead of Noble, so it had been filed under the wrong letter of the alphabet." If you didn't pronounce mobile like the British did when referring to their cell phones, and instead pronounced it so it rhymed with noble, I could see how the midwife might have made an honest mistake in her recording of the dictation.

"We learned she had been adopted, but it was a closed adoption, as most were in those days, and it took another year to get the records unsealed. She had been adopted by a couple called Michael and Mary Johnson. Finnick hired a private detective to find the Johnsons, but they had left the area. Did you know Johnson is the most common last name in America? More common than Smith or Jones, and don't get me started on the commonness of Mary or Michael. In the years to come, the detectives chased down dozens of people named Michael Johnson who had adopted a baby around the time Elowen was born. Remember, there was no Google back then."

"But you did find her?" I said firmly as I took a bite of my pancakes.

"They had changed her name to Eleanor, something about it being more down to earth than Elowen, and moved several times. It took years and a string of private investigators just to discover those things. Finally, Finnick and I hit upon the idea of using an investigator who was also a Witch. It was a novel profession for our kind at the time. I had the pacifier, and because it had Elowen's DNA on it; we didn't call it DNA then, but you understand... The right kind of Witch could use it to build a tracking spell. Hair, blood, saliva, skin cells, all those things can be used in a finding spell. Private investigators who are also Witches are quite rare, so it took us ages to find one."

"That's where I come in," volunteered Westley Thindrell, my grandfather.

Chapter 6

"Before I start, you must understand, when I was hired, I didn't know any of the background. I was 20 years old, and just starting out as a private eye for magical beings," he contemplated for a second and then added rakishly, "and mighty good at what I did." He twirled one end of his whiskers then winked at me, and I got the impression dark-furred Westley had been a handsome, cavalier, self-assured young Warlock.

"All I knew was I was being paid to find this adopted girl because her biological family had left her a fortune. I tracked Elowen to Oregon. She had just turned 18. Poor kid. Her powers had started to manifest when she was 16. They were weak because she had lived so far from the Mountain most of her life, and her powers were not the same as a normal Witch. She was a telepath and a clairvoyant. Try telling human parents you hear other people's thoughts and see visions of the future. Among humans, if you hear things and see things that aren't there, all you get is a trip to the psychiatrist and a fist full of antipsychotics. The pills gave her a foggy-brained feeling for over two years, and she didn't like it at all. She still heard the voices sometimes and every now and then was able to discern a nonhuman in their true form. She genuinely thought she was insane.

"It took me a few weeks to gain her trust, but I convinced her she was a Witch, and she needed to stop taking the medication. I taught her a little magic, and a bit about controlling her powers." He paused and looked wistful, casting a bashful glance in my direction. "She was so beautiful. She looked rather like Snow White, from the fairy tale, you know?"

"Don't they all," I grumbled under my breath letting my jealousy show. If she even remotely resembled Reverie and Mother, I could see a theme beginning to emerge: blue eyes, dark hair, red lips, and creamy skin.

"So," he continued reluctantly, "A romance ensued. Her parents didn't like me much, so our meetings were usually on the sly, but hey, she was an adult." Westley seemed unusually defensive when telling this part of the story. I looked at the other pikas to see if I could pick up something, but they had both chosen this moment to examine their tiny paws.

"I told her about the house and the money she had inherited, and we decided to elope and come here for our honeymoon."

"Yes," commented Ric dourly. "He left out the part about eloping when he talked to Finnick on the phone. Westley just told my attorney he had found the girl, and they were on their way home."

"Mr. Grey, that's Finnick," Westley offered in an aside, in case I was losing track of all the characters in this bizarre drama, "gave me directions to this house, and we arranged a time to meet here. We were traveling from Oregon in an unreliable clunker of a car and arrived very late the night before the meeting was to take place, and finding the door opened... Now, remember it was her house... We came in and slept here."

"Zeke and I were asleep downstairs when they arrived and didn't hear them come in," commented Ric.

Westley continued sheepishly, "Elowen must have conceived the girls that night because I woke up in our bed the next morning as a pika, and she was screaming her head off."

To be fair, if I woke up with a mouse-like creature in my bed, you'd have been able to hear my screams in Montana.

"Wait, wait," I said, "Go back, you said *girls* plural."

"Demelza and I," offered Reverie as if this were common knowledge, but I was obviously severely lacking in knowledge of this particular facet of the family tree. In fact, *my tree* was in a whole different forest.

"No, no, that can't be right. Mother is at least 12 or 15 years older than you." I stammered, wondering if *I* might need antipsychotic drugs before this was all over.

"Your mother and I are identical twins. Remember, Witches only have one pregnancy. I look younger than I am in human years. Demelza looks older because she has chosen to live far away from the Mountain for so long, and she doesn't practice magic. People probably tell her she looks young for her age, and she does, but in comparison, she has aged more rapidly," supplied Reverie.

"Okay, okay. Hold on for just one minute," I exclaimed in irritation directing my words to Westley. I found I was repeating words a great deal, "So you were married for how long before you went all furry and abandoned this woman? All of two days?"

"Four days," he remarked sheepishly, "But I DIDN'T KNOW!"

"Is she alright?" Ric asked my aunt, nodding towards me. "She looks a little dazed."

"It's a huge amount of information to take in all at once. I don't think she's ready for your part yet," she inclined her head towards my father. "I better take over for a while."

They all bobbed their heads in agreement. I glowered at them. I was sitting right here! No need to act as if I couldn't hear their conversation.

"Ric and Zeke and later Finnick, when he arrived, tried to explain the situation to my mom and to Westley, because let's face it, he was a victim, too, but she didn't take it very well, as you can imagine. Never in his wildest dreams did Finnick think Westley would marry

Elowen before he could explain the Curse to her, and in those days, they weren't sure the Curse was generational. Everybody was in new territory here.

"Elowen was an untrained Witch, and there wasn't anybody here who could train her. She learned what she could from the books and journals of her mom, Lorelei, and the advice of the pikas, but she struggled and was lonely. Finnick hired round the clock Fae nurses to stay here when the time grew close for our birth, and he also kept close at hand. Nobody wanted a repeat of Elowen's birth.

"After we were born, my mother totally lost her zest for life. Her adopted parents had disowned her when they found out she was pregnant and had no husband."

"What am I, chopped liver?" asked Westley of me imploringly.

I shrugged apologetically. I had known an old lady who fed chopped liver to her cats, but it seemed tacky to share this information, him being a form of live cat food and all. Reverie ignored his outburst and continued her narrative.

"Some days, she stayed in bed, and other days, she would wander the Mountain for hours, seemingly in a haze. The Pixies were charged with keeping an eye on her, but one good thing began to happen, since she was physically present, the Mountain and the inhabitants started to thrive again, and this fact alone gave her life more purpose than anything else she had experienced, even her own children." By children, she meant herself and Mother. It was a dismal indictment of their childhood.

"Ric and Westley, along with Zeke, practically raised us. That's why I call them by their first names, I didn't know until I turned six that the pikas were my father and grandfather. They taught us to read and do math and other stuff. After our powers manifested, when we were 10, Finnick enrolled us in a local school for Witches."

She must have seen the gleam in my eyes because she continued rather quickly, "And, no, it was nothing like Hogwarts. It was a 20-minute drive up the canyon in a small town called Heber City. We only had about 13 students. The school provided education for all the Witching communities in the state. It was a new experiment then, run by three of the remaining Witches who had previously lived on the Mountain, and it has since failed and gone out of business. Finnick would drop us off on Monday morning and would come and get us on Friday afternoons. We boarded there during the week. Demelza was excellent at the human part of the curriculum, especially the sciences, but she never excelled at the magic. She was convinced she could reverse the Curse if she could figure out its genetic structure on a cellular level."

"So, that's what she's been working on all these years?" Mother's obsession was starting to make more sense. Then I remembered the biomedical package. "You send her samples of their blood for her research," I said to Reverie, indicating the pikas.

"From time to time," she confirmed, "My own blood, too. I think she uses her own as well." Maybe mine, too, I thought remembering the yearly 'check-ups' where she had drawn my blood.

"Alright, your turn." I glared at Dr. Vinn Everton, my father, the not-mouse.

The mostly cinnamon colored pika cleared his throat nervously.

"I have duel doctorate degrees in Physics and Astronomy. Your mother and I both had grants at the same research facility. I never knew exactly what she was researching, but I knew it had something to do with isolating a specific gene that caused a particular disorder."

"Astronomy?" I asked with thoughtful suspicion. "I have a poster of a three-dimensional model of a famous asteroid cluster. In my earliest memories, it has always been in my room no matter where we lived. Does that have something to do with you?"

"I had Reverie send you it for your second birthday," he blushed and seemed very pleased. "I always sent you something for Christmas and for your birthday." I eyed my aunt distrustfully. Mother told me the gifts came from Reverie. Had Mother deceived me, or had my aunt? I suspected it had been Mother.

"Your mother never displayed any unusual abilities, so I didn't know she was a Witch, and she didn't know I was a Warlock. I'm not all that powerful myself," he confessed bashfully, "It's not something you converse with people about in the real world. I mean, it's easy to see through the glamour of Naiads and Hags and other nonhuman things, but Witches pretty much look like ordinary people. The Witching community is small, and I had never heard of your family. Most super naturals avoid big cities and live in isolated communities like this one, so I didn't expect a Witch to be working at a research facility in New York City. It is also rare for a Witch's power to be tied so specifically to a place like the Mountain."

I was relatively sure this was leading up to something, but I couldn't quite figure out what I was missing. Reverie saw my confusion and stepped in to help me out.

"Remember yesterday when I told you we can mate with humans, but we can only produce offspring with another of our kind?" She prompted gently. I nodded, light beginning to dawn.

"Well," continued Vinn. "We had an affair. We never lived together, but we dated for almost a year. I wanted her to marry me, but she just laughed and said it wouldn't be fair to me; she was married to her work. Now, I realize she didn't think she could have a child with me because she thought I was human, and the Curse could have no effect in that case, but one morning, I woke up here looking like this." The morning after my conception, if history held true.

"Does Mother know you're here?" I asked timidly, suddenly feeling much more sympathetic towards him. He had gotten a raw deal of mammoth proportion. He was trapped in this place, so he could never have lived with me, even if he'd wanted to. I had judged him unfairly.

"Yes, of course," assured Reverie. "I called her the minute he showed up, and just like Ric and Westley if he tries to leave, he ends up right back here."

I looked down. My pancakes were stone cold, and I had only eaten a few bites, a fact I did not recall.

"Your mother took care of all the loose ends, so no one became suspicious of Vinn's disappearance. She cancelled his lease and packed up his apartment, then explained the situation to his parents and sent them his belongings. She even wrote emails to his employer from his computer requesting a leave of absence due to the sudden onset of a serious illness, and later resigned for him." I was sure getting turned into a rodent (or whatever they were, insert my imaginary eyeroll— here) wouldn't be covered by health insurance.

I sat in silence for a few beats. Finally, I concluded that if I ever wanted my family to be together and have a "normal" life, we needed to break this Curse, but how? Judging from the abundance of doctorate degrees in my gene pool, I was a brainy girl, right?

"So," I asked, thinking like the daughter of two scientists. "If Lorelei was close to breaking this Curse 50-plus years ago before she died in childbirth, then why hasn't one of you been able to finish undoing it? Didn't she leave notes on her research?"

"Well, that's just it, after Lorelei died," stated Ric, "Finnick Grey, Zeke, and I searched this house from top to bottom. Jasper's grimoire and all of Lorelei's notes were nowhere to be found."

Chapter 7

"Alright," Reverie remarked in a get-down-to business tone, "there is absolutely nothing we can do about the Curse today, and Lyric and I have important work to do." The pikas grumbled, but after my aunt assured them there would be ample time to get to know me over the summer, they agreed to retire and allow us to get busy with our magic lessons.

"I'm really sorry," she offered sincerely as I followed her to her workshop, "You have to believe I fully intended to tell you about your father and the other pikas once you got settled in. I told them to keep out of sight until then. I just really didn't expect you to be up so early. Do you still want to call your mom?"

I wasn't sure if I was ready to talk to her, even if she did have her phone turned on in the middle of the night, which was unlikely. I was angry and hurt. She had lied to me and kept my father's existence a secret. I shook my head negatively. At some point, when I had time alone to process all the thoughts and emotions whirling around in my brain, I would confront Mother.

When we arrived in the attic, I noticed Reverie had placed several objects of varying sizes and weights on the table, including a feather, a pen, a book, a pillow, and an iron. There was a Brownie plumping pillows on the chairs in the sitting area. I knew he was a Brownie because he looked exactly as Reverie had described, about two feet tall, brown gnarled skin, spiky hair, and green eyes. His only clothing was a clean, sleeveless, tan linen tunic which came to his knees and was tied around the waist with a belt of braided hemp.

"Lyric, this is Zeke, our house Brownie," she said with a warm smile.

"Pleased to meet you, Miss. I'm sorry I didn't get in to see you last night at dinner, but I was babysitting my pie, didn't want to burn the best part of the meal," said Zeke cheerfully with a small bow before turning to Reverie. "I'm just going to go around and wipe the baseboards while I'm up here if that's alright with you, Miss Reverie. I haven't done them in a while. Don't let me disturb your lesson. I'll be out of your way before you know it."

"Sure, Zeke, whatever you need to do," responded Reverie nonchalantly before seating herself at the table, kicking off her shoes, and turning her attention to me.

"I thought we'd start with telekinesis. You already have some talent with manipulating objects, because you're doing it in the sub-consciousness of your dream world. When you dream of flying, objects around you float, too. When you knocked Madison down, you referred to it as energy going out of you. Moving objects or people with your mind is like pushing energy away from you or pulling it towards you. I want to see how much control you have before we decide what to do next. Witches sometimes use different objects to help focus their powers; a wand, a staff, a talisman, and even a familiar. Have you heard of a familiar?"

"Isn't it an animal that can be used to channel more power? That's why Witches always have a black cat in the stories, right?"

"Yes, except no cats allowed in this house." She gave me a knowing look.

"The pikas?" I laughed.

"Exactly," she said as she tapped the side of her forehead, indicating I was a quick thinker.

"I need to know specifically what sort of focus object you need, or if you even need one at all. The most talented Witches can perform spells without using them."

"Yes, but I don't know how to move things with my conscious mind," I stammered uneasily while panic rose in my chest.

"I know, that's why I'm here," she reassured me calmly. "Now, have you ever done karate or yoga or some other far eastern disciplinary practice?"

"Yes," I scoffed, thinking of the endless lessons. "Pretty much all of the above." Not that I had been good at any of them, but I kept that last bit to myself.

"So, you're familiar with the practice of relaxing and centering yourself?" I nodded, and she continued, "Sit in one of those armchairs, move it to squarely face the table, find a comfortable position, and do some deep breathing."

After I had complied, she went on, "Now, think of your magic as a force that lives within you. Here." She tapped me lightly on my breastbone. "At first, it will be important to try and picture it as something concrete with living energy like a campfire, or a waterfall. Later, with enough practice, you will automatically go to your power supply without having to think so hard. Now, focus on the supply of energy and try to push it outward, so you can lift the smallest and lightest of the objects on the table. You can close your eyes if it helps you concentrate."

I closed my eyes and tried to picture the energy behind my sternum. When I touched upon it, I inhaled sharply with surprise. It felt more like a core of molten lava than a cozy campfire or bubbly spring. On my next inhale, I pictured grabbing the lava, and on my exhale, I thought of pushing it out through my fingertips.

When I heard Reverie's sudden intake of breath and a terrified squeal from the corner of the room, my eyes flew open in alarm. All the objects were floating three feet off the table and when I lost my concentration they slammed violently down onto the tabletop, except the pen, which rolled onto the floor, and the feather, which wafted slowly back to earth a moment later. I was also stunned to realize I had thrown my right hand forward, palm up, even though I didn't remember moving.

When I swiveled my head in the direction of the squeal, I found Zeke, back pressed against the wall, white knuckled fingers clutching his feather duster and eyes as wide as silver dollars. Making a conscious effort to close his hanging jaw, he colored deeply and reluctantly turned his back on us to continue his work. The next time I looked in his direction, he was nowhere to be found. Great, I was so bad at this I had caused the house Brownie to flee in terror.

"Okaaay, maybe back off just a tad on the amount of thrust," observed Reverie slowly with more than a hint of sarcasm before continuing seriously, "I knew you were strong, but I have to admit I'm surprised. That's the most power I've ever seen in a newbie."

The second effort was better. This time only the pen, feather and pillow rose. Over the course of the morning, I learned raw power was a good thing, but power without control was a recipe for disaster. Reverie had me practice again and again, first with eyes closed and then, as I gained some control, with open eyes.

"Closing your eyes might increase your concentration at first, but if you have to continue to close your eyes every time you cast a spell, you will be blind to enemy attacks and make yourself vulnerable to extreme danger."

Yikes! What kind of enemy attacks? Reverie had said nothing about anything dangerous living on the Mountain. Who would want to hurt me anyway? I was just a scrawny teenager who wanted to learn magic to get back at some bullies, but that's when I realized this wasn't a frivolous teenage diversion. It was a serious responsibility. I ground my teeth, and I doubled my efforts. I was determined to be good at this, no matter what it took.

Ultimately, I could lift each object on command, but then she made me practice hovering each to a specific height. Lastly, once airborne, she wanted to see if I could push the things away or pull them toward myself. She kept using phrases like "funnel the energy," "narrow your focus," and "taper the flow." I was successful about 75 percent of the time, but there were some epic failures, and even when I did succeed, my control would often waiver. Reverie seemed encouraged and assured me I would become an expert with more practice. I wasn't sure if I believed her.

After several hours, I was exhausted, and a slight headache was beginning to form behind my right eye. My hair, the bane of my existence, hung limply around my face. Unlike Mother and Reverie, who had thick luxurious hair, mine was fine and thin. If I cut it too short, it stuck out like kitten fur, and if I let it get too long, the ends would split and break, making me look truly like a stereotypical witch. If it was hot outside or if I exerted myself at all, my nondescript, medium-length, medium-brown hair became lank and stringy.

I sagged with relief when I heard the chimes sounding to call us to lunch, or what I fervently hoped was lunch, because I had been working extremely hard, and my breakfast had been abandoned during the pikas' saga. Reverie gave me a long, evaluating look before reaching for one of many jars filled with herbs and potions. She opened the bottle, shook out two white tablets, and handed them to me. I raised my eyebrows inquiringly. I didn't want to unknowingly swallow crystalized goat urine or concentrated cow drool.

"Aspirin," she chuckled reassuringly at my reluctance. "I think that's enough for one day. You'd better take it easy this afternoon. No one has infinite magic reserves, and you're a beginner.

"Never completely drain your reserves, no matter how motivated you are to excel. Doing too much can leave you unable to perform even the simplest of menial tasks," she warned, somehow inherently knowing I often pushed myself with unreasonable expectations of perfection.

"You need food and a diversion to restore you." She handed me another textbook called *Tools of Witchcraft*. "Read the chapter on candles for tomorrow. I think maybe we'll walk down to *The Art Hut* once we've eaten."

A delicious lunch of perfectly toasted grilled cheese sandwiches, potato chips, and homemade chocolate chip cookies was waiting for us in the kitchen, but Zeke was not in attendance. Reverie seemed to be expecting him at any moment, but the little Brownie never appeared. Her brows furrowed in consternation, but she held her tongue on the subject.

After we had eaten our fill, we set off down the lane in the opposite direction from the way we had come from the airport yesterday. It was cool and shady and mostly downhill, so we clipped along with little effort.

"Tell me about our family's ties to the Mountain," I asked Reverie. I was thirsty for knowledge about this place, my family, and anything else that might be helpful in breaking the Curse. Mother had always told me I needed to gather all the facts before I made my first hypothesis.

"Long ago, there were Native Americans who lived on the Mountain," she began, and the verbiage and cadence of her language took on the tone of a story that had been repeated for generations.

"They sacrificed to the great god Timpanogos. One year, there was a drought, and the people thought the great god was angry with them. The chief of this tribe had a beautiful daughter who was of age to be chosen for the sacrifice. All the girls of that age were asked to choose a pebble from a pottery dish. They were blindfolded, so no one had an advantage. The chief's daughter, Utahna, chose the black pebble, which meant it was her fate to go to the top of the Mountain and cast herself off the highest peak as the tribal sacrifice.

"All of her tribesmen were devastated and wanted someone else to go instead, but she was devout and took her duty seriously, so she ascended, winding her way towards the summit of Mount Timpanogos.

"When she reached the top, she knelt in prayer. She made her plea to the god of Timpanogos, begging for rain, with her arms outstretched towards the heavens. A handsome young brave of another tribe, who was out hunting, had caught a glimpse of the beautiful maiden and followed her to the top out of curiosity. His name was Red Eagle, and he pleaded with her not to jump. Utahna thought Red Eagle was the great god of Timpanogos answering her prayer. He led her to Timpanogos Cave, his hunting shelter, and there they lived in love and devotion to one another.

"One day, Red Eagle was attacked by a cougar. Since he was injured, Utahna realized he was not the great god of Timpanogos, because a god would have been invincible. She nursed him back to health, then left to ascend the Mountain and completed her sacrifice.

"When the sun came up, she threw herself onto the crags below. Realizing too late where she had gone, Red Eagle found and gathered her broken body in his arms and carried her to their cave. He brooded over her body and was almost reduced to madness until the true god of Timpanogos had mercy upon him and joined their bleeding hearts into one, charging them to become protectors of the Mountain forever. In Timpanogos Cave, a few miles from here, there is a huge stalactite known as 'The Great Heart.' It resembles two hearts that have been fused into one.

"It is said that Red Eagle was immortalized in the spirit of Emerald Lake located in a lonely mountain valley above us, and if you look closely at the top of Mount Timpanogos, you can see the outline of Utahna's profile as she lays stretched out across the ridge top, her arms folded across her chest. Their conjoined hearts placed deep inside the Mountain are said to be the lifeblood of this area. He controls the elements of water and earth, and she controls air and fire. Together they maintain balance.

"When my family first settled here in the early nineteenth century, Utahna's spirit contacted my great-great grandmother and made a promise to her. If my ancestor and her female descendants would watch over the Mountain and make sacrifices of their time and talents for the good of the inhabitants, they would receive strength and power, and the princess' protection, and so it has been from that time until this day."

For the rest of our walk, we didn't talk much as I contemplated the story, but Reverie, always the teacher, occasionally pointed out a plant in the dense undergrowth with useful magical properties. We walked for about a mile and saw 15 or 20 houses scattered along the way before we passed the log cabin marked Riverwynd Spa, and our road ended abruptly at a parallel crossroad. At this three-way stop, we left Riverwynd Drive, crossed the new street called Hilda's Way. Then we made our way down a flight of stairs cut into the rocky hillside lined with railroad ties, entered a narrow, paved footpath that meandered along, and crossed a small bridge over the brook. Eventually, we came to the back service entrance to the Riverwynd Resort.

There were several rusty tin-roofed, graying barn-wood structures scattered about to carefully cultivate the ambiance of an old mining town. Although the buildings were neither abandoned nor dilapidated, they had been crafted to give that appearance, almost as if they were scenery props built on the backlot of a movie set. A ticket booth with attached chair lift, ski and mountain biking paraphernalia store, summer outdoor amphitheater, offices, expensive gift shop, a small hotel lobby where you could rent cabins owned by the resort, and restaurants were located in buildings to the right with the art buildings across an employee parking lot to the left. The stream spilled over a small, rocky waterfall into a manmade pond, around which some of the buildings picturesquely clustered, before continuing on its winding way under a few charming wooden bridges, and in between the remaining resort edifices before plunging down alongside the mountain roadway to eventually merge with the Provo River.

We walked by the glass blowing area as we headed for the entrance to *The Art Hut*. The structure reminded me of an oversized crèche where you display your manger scene at Christmas time. Along the back wall were an annealing oven and two fiery hot furnaces. The other three sides were open to the air with waist high railings, so bystanders could watch without getting in the way of the craftsmen or wandering too close to the ovens, and for ventilation to allow the scorching heat to escape. I counted four barrel-chested, well-muscled Dwarfs busily at work.

Allegra, who was dressed more like a modern-day shop keeper today in navy pants and a tailored white shirt, with her hair braided and coiled around her head in a style that would give Princess Leia a run for her money, was just hanging up the telephone as the bell over the door jingled when we entered the tiny art gallery. She stood behind a high counter where she kept the phone, cash register, and supplies for wrapping fragile purchases.

"That was Viktor on the phone," she remarked to Reverie. "Indigo got too close to a mare about to foal and was bitten on the flank. The mare's teeth broke her hide. He can't leave the stable because the colt's birth is imminent, and the mare is presenting breach. He called your house, and Zeke told him you were on the way here. He was wondering if you could come take a look at Indigo's wound and maybe help with the foaling."

"Viktor and Indigo Wilde are Centaurs," said Reverie to me by way of information. I remembered a Centaur was a half-human, half-horse. "They work at the Riverwynd Stables with regular riding horses in the summertime. Indigo is Viktor's teenage daughter." She turned to Allegra with a concerned look on her face.

"It will take too long to walk. I can teleport myself there, but I can't take Lyric with me. We haven't covered teleportation yet, and it would be too dangerous for her to cross the Everafter without experience."

Allegra looked wary. I could tell she wasn't comfortable being responsible for a teenager all afternoon. "I have a completely full pottery class to teach in about 30 minutes."

I looked around. The art studio was tiny. There was nothing here for me to do if Allegra was occupied.

"Don't worry about me," I volunteered hurriedly, "I can get home by myself. I remember the way." Allegra seemed visibly relieved. She took her class responsibilities very seriously.

Reverie eyed me closely looking for signs of uncertainty before asking, "Are you sure?"

"Yes, of course." I was an expert at reassuring adults about my well-being. "Cross the parking lot, along the path, up the stairs, across the street and up the lane until I see the home of..." here I switched to the tune of a popular Christmas carol, "...three American pikas, two zany Witches, and a Kitsune...uh, in a pear tree?" I finished lamely.

"You left out the Brownie," Reverie chuckled. Allegra harrumphed, but I saw a twinkle in her eye even though she pretended not to be amused at my makeshift jingle.

"Oh, yeah, I forgot," I commented with a self-conscious shrug.

"I'll give her a little tour first, since you walked all this way," proposed Allegra. The offer was a kind gesture to alleviate my aunt's apprehension, but at the same time, she was attempting to sooth her own conscience about having to abandon me.

"Okay, I'll be off then," said Reverie as she performed that little gesture with her right wrist, spun in a clockwise direction and was gone. I think there might have even been a puff of smoke, but maybe I imagined it.

"Wow!" I exclaimed as I raised my eyebrows at Allegra.

"Rather dramatic if you ask me, but Witches do like a bit of theatrics," Allegra commented in a voice that was less than impressed, clicking her tongue and shaking her head. "Now, where should we start?"

As I had stated, the gallery was small. There were some watercolor and oil paintings of local landscapes displayed on the walls and some plinths containing pottery and glass sculptures scattered around the room. A few shelving units lining the walls under the paintings showed smaller pottery pieces and baskets filled with soaps. A bay window also contained a selection of blown glass Christmas ornaments hanging from fishing line attached to the ceiling, the sunlight making them sparkle and cast prisms of light on the surrounding surfaces. On one side of the room, I noticed a door and a large plate glass window with a view into an adjoining studio.

"What's in there?" I asked.

"That's Briar's soap making domain. She's not here today because it's Friday, and she only makes soap on Monday and Thursday." I peered through the glass. The equipment in the studio reminded me of a bakery or candy making factory. It was immaculately clean, and an aroma of fresh plants wafted under the door. There was a large, marble topped table, stainless steel mixing vats and racks of plastic bins containing neatly labeled dried herbs and what I assumed were other soap making ingredients.

The only thing organic in the sea of sterility was a meticulously pruned bonsai tree proudly displayed on the drain board of the stainless-steel sink. It was planted in an amber-colored, blown glass bowl. The glass bowl sat in an outer sculptural vessel made of metal. The metal was either silver or pewter. It resembled several gnarled tree trunks with sprawling roots for feet and lacy, curving, intertwined branches for cradling the inner glass bowl. The golden color of the blown glass peeked thru the delicate filigree of the metal branches reminiscent of fall foliage. It was too far away to really see the details, but I could tell it was exquisite.

"What can you tell me about Briar?" I asked with a furrowed brow. I regretted falling asleep so early last night. I had meant to find out more about Dryads. I needed to learn all I could about the inhabitants of the community.

"A Dryad is the spirit of an oak tree. We don't have many oaks here, so she is a rarity in this area. She considers herself a spokesman for the forest. She takes care of the plants and trees while your aunt cares for the other creatures on the Mountain. The Pixies help her find the herbs for her soaps. She donates most of the money she makes from the soap to environmental causes."

"She seems like an interesting person," I commented politely, hoping for more information.

"She's shy and a bit irresponsible when it comes to things that are not plant related." In my short time knowing Allegra, I had found her to be prim and outdated in many of her customs and mannerisms, but also refreshingly, if not brutally, honest. "Come along, and I'll show you my studio. I'm teaching a class for some resort guests at 2:00, if it wasn't full, I'd invite you to join us. If they all show up, it will be tight quarters."

Through a door hung with strands of multi-colored beads across from Briar's viewing window sat five industrial looking metal stools behind five pottery wheels on a polished cement floor with a large porcelain sink to one side, and metal shelves containing pottery waiting to be fired, mixed with some completed pieces. In one corner, I noticed the kiln. Dusty remnants of dried gray clay splattered the floor, the walls, the sink and everything else. Like the elements of Pandora's Box, clay was one of those messy mediums not easily gotten rid of once it was introduced into an environment.

"I would really love to take one of your classes sometime," I said wistfully. Art was comforting. It allowed me to think and to process my feelings.

"I have an opening on Monday afternoon. Why don't I put you down, so we can make sure you have a reserved spot?" I agreed and went back to the main gallery, so she could write my name in her appointment book behind the counter. "I have a few minutes before my class, let's go out to the glass blowing studio and watch the Trams."

The Dwarfs were busy making a set of green glass goblets. Each had their own job, gathering, blowing, reheating, shaping, cooling, and beginning the process over again like an intricate dance. It was mesmerizing to watch. As they were too busy to talk, Allegra explained the process and told me about the Dwarfs as they worked.

"Heath Tram is the father, a classically trained master glass blower. His wife, Poloma, was a blacksmith before they met, the two things have some similarities, so Heath taught Poloma to do glass work. The other two are their grown sons and apprentices, Asa and Atlas."

During a break in the process, the female Dwarf wandered over to get a drink from a jug of water stored close to where Allegra and I were standing. She was about a foot shorter than I, with a stocky body and sharp, hawk-like facial features. She was not especially attractive, and the only way to tell her from the male Dwarfs was her beardless face. Her hair was plastered to her head with perspiration. She was having a worse hair day than me, and that was something I didn't even think was possible, but she didn't seem to care. She ripped protective goggles off her head as she came towards us. Over her cargo pants and long-sleeved t-shirt, she wore heavy gloves and a thick leather apron to protect her from burns. Her feet were encased in clunky, steel-toed combat boots.

"This is Poloma Tram," stated Allegra.

"Oh, hello," I beamed and then blurted out a sudden thought, "Did you make that gorgeous sculpture of trees holding Briar's bonsai?" Poloma shot Allegra a cagey glance and eyed me suspiciously.

"This is Lyric Thindrell, Demelza's daughter. I told her you used to be a blacksmith. She's a budding artist herself," supplied Allegra.

"Yes, I made it," she replied taciturnly to answer my question, after which she shrugged her shoulders and mumbled, "I'd better get back to work."

"Don't take it personally," offered Allegra softly, "Dwarfs are a bit distrustful and gruff with everyone." We noticed a group of people approaching from the other side of the parking lot. "That will be my class."

As I was thanking Allegra for her time, so I could hurriedly say goodbye before her students arrived, she formally invited, "I only work until noon tomorrow. Would you be my guest for afternoon tea in my apartment at 3:00?"

"I would be honored," I replied with a grateful smile. It was nice to have a friend, even if she was an elderly fox-lady.

The walk home was much more strenuous going up than it had been coming down, so I found myself trudging slowly along and stopping often to catch my breath and take in the glorious scenery. A flock of wild turkeys meandered across the road in front of me shortly after I passed the spa. Though they were probably common in this setting, I was quite awestruck and found them to be amazing. I stood stock still as they passed, hardly daring to breathe as I tried not to startle them; however, they were unimpressed and unfazed by my presence. I had never seen so much wildlife this close at hand.

So, my father did exist after all, I thought as I resumed my plodding uphill course. What could I do to break this Curse? Everyone involved seemed to have been trying for a very long time with no luck. Mother always said if your hypothesis proved false, then you were asking the wrong questions. Perhaps all that was needed was a fresh prospective. To slow my heart rate, I wandered off the road a few times to get a better look at some of the plants Reverie had pointed out on our way down and to think. Everything was jumbled up in my head. I thought about the weirdness of meeting my pika father, the thrill of my magic lesson this morning, the hominess of *The Art Hut* and Mother's utter deception about everything in my life. How was it possible to feel elated and peaceful one second and hurt and confused the next?

During one of my forays into the forest, I was startled by the sharp sound of a branch breaking right behind me. I jumped involuntarily, my heart giving one loud thud before I whirled to find myself staring at a terrifying specter of a woman just inches away. Talk about no respect for personal space, she was hovering way too close for comfort. She was tall, extremely thin, and wore a long, tattered, hooded, black choir robe. Her black hair was knotted and messy with twigs in it. The scariest thing was her eerily unfocused milky white eyes with no visible irises or pupils. My heart hammered an adrenaline-laced staccato, and fear clenched in my belly.

"Pleeese," screeched her mournfully pleading wail, "Bring back my love!"

Chapter 8

My first instinct was to get as far away from this creature as fast as my feet would carry me. I backpedaled a few steps before tripping over a stump and falling onto the loamy leaves and dirt of the forest floor. As the woman started to reach towards me, I wanted to throw power at her, but I realized the last time I had attempted this course of action the consequences had not turned out well for me, so I hesitated. That's when I noticed a swarm of perfectly proportioned, human-shaped creatures no more than two inches tall with iridescent dragonfly wings hurtling to my rescue.

"Hurry, Cursebreaker... Please, you must hurry," the woman begged in an eerily hollow voice, her vacant eyes painfully desperate.

"Elowen! Elowen!" the little folks chorused in their tiny shrill voices, trying to distract the woman. She slowly turned her head towards the sounds, and as she did, her eyes lost their lifeless quality and resumed the features of normal eyes with black pupils and bright blue irises, although she still seemed dazed and confused.

"Sit on this stump until you regain your strength, Elowen," chirped one of the Pixies who seemed to be in charge. The woman sat staring into the middle distance.

"Cami," the head Pixie continued, "go and tell Dara we found Elowen in the woods by Kilrawk."

"Yes, Clementine," called golden-haired Cami as she zipped away, her wings a blur.

"What's Kilrawk? Who's Dara? Wait... Wait... Wait! What do you mean, Elowen?" I stammered.

"This baby Witch asks a lot of stupid questions," remarked another Pixie with disdain.

"Cora," scolded the leader, "This is rude behavior. The little Witch is obviously a stranger here and has had quite a scare."

"From Elowen?" laughed another Pixie with evident mirth, "But, Elowen is harmless."

"Yes, but she does not know this, Cozy. Elowen can be frightening to look upon when she is taken with the second sight." The gaggle of fluttering Pixies all nodded in agreement.

"Please, will someone tell me what is going on?" I pleaded for the second time today.

"My name is Clementine," said the lead Pixie slowly as if I were a three-year-old, "That house in the clearing behind you is called Kil-rawk. It's named after a castle in Scotland. See the name chiseled in letters on the large boulder at the head of the driveway? And Dara is Elowen's caretaker. This," she pointed to the woman now sitting do-cilely on the stump staring into space ignoring me and everything around her as if she were on drugs, "is Elowen."

"No," I stated as a matter of fact, "Elowen is dead."

"This is an untruth. Who told you this?" asked Clementine, a tiny frown marring her perfect features. I considered it for a moment. Who had told me my grandmother was dead? Well, no one.

"I think I just assumed," I admitted meekly. If she wasn't dead, why didn't she live with Reverie and her pika husband, Westley?

"Ah," replied Clementine sagely. "It is never safe to assume."

"So," I stated as I confirmed my thoughts out loud, "Elowen does-n't live with Reverie."

"No, Elowen has her own small cottage, on the lane, there." She pointed to an almost hidden dirt track across the road from where Elowen and I were sitting, "She prefers it that way. She's calmer if there are not too many of the thoughts of others intruding on her own.

She is what Witches call a hermit, like the great Merlin, but Reverie has charged us to look after her, for she sometimes wanders away from Dara. Pixies make good guards."

"And spies," added Cora proudly.

"And alarm systems," volunteered Cozy.

"And finders," chimed a male Pixie. Yes, that rang a bell, hadn't Allegra said they found herbs for Briar's soaps?

"And secret keepers," whispered another Pixie conspiratorially, with a wink. Finders? Secret keepers? Maybe they knew something about Jasper's missing grimoire. It seemed to be part of the key to unraveling this Curse business.

"Did you know Lorelei?" I asked as the thought struck me.

"Lorelei, Elowen's mother?" asked Clementine. I nodded. "No, Pixies only live about 25 human years. Lorelei died well over 50 years ago." She must have seen the disappointment register on my face because she hurriedly continued, "But we have what is called collective knowledge." Just then, a female version of Zeke came rushing our way.

"Oh, I'm just so sorry, I am, you must be Miss Lyric," she cooed as she smiled broadly, "She must have given you quite the fright, then, didn't she? She does like to wander when the visions are upon her. Where are my manners, now? I'm Dara, Zeke's cousin." The Pixie, Cami, who had been sent to collect Dara, came winging in and rejoined the collective.

"It's nice to meet you," I said as my own manners kicked in. "Zeke and I haven't spoken much. He has been rather shy around me."

"Shy? Our Zeke? Well, that's a funny one," she chortled before turning to speak gently to the figure sitting on the stump.

"Oh, Miss Elowen, must you insist on wearing these rags?" she chided kindly as she took my grandmother's hand, "You know, you have perfectly good clothes at home, and what have you done to your hair? Been chasing wild pikas in the thorn bushes again, have you? Come along now, let's get you home and cleaned up." Elowen allowed the little Brownie to lead her away, but just before they were lost from view, she turned and gave me a totally sane, soul piercing gaze, causing me to shudder.

After a few seconds, I pushed myself up off the ground, brushed the leaves and dirt from my clothes as best I could, and made my way to the road to continue home. The cloud of colorful Pixies followed. The females were clothed in gauzy, pearlescent, short dresses with uneven hems, in shades of pink, turquoise, lavender, and mint while the males, reminiscent of Peter Pan, wore dark green tunics made from soft felt. All had hair the color of spun gold, all were barefoot, and all carried miniscule weapons, either a crossbow with a quiver of tiny arrows, a sword strapped to their backs, or a deadly looking spear held at the ready by their sides.

"What is collective knowledge?" I asked Clementine.

"On the whole, Pixies may live for an average of 25 human years, give or take a few years, but our knowledge is passed from generation to generation through a bit of magic and memorized oral storytelling traditions. We store the history and secrets of the families we are charged to look after, bound by blood oaths."

"Sorry," I apologized. "What is a blood oath?"

"You really are a baby Witch," she observed, but not unkindly. "As Clove stated earlier, Pixies are secret keepers, a special burden and power we were given when we were first created by a Witch's spell. Where there are Witches, there will always be Pixies. In days gone by, when feudal lords and magical creatures waged epic battles, it was crucial for secrets to pass back and forth during campaigns. We were used as a tool of war to be spies, giving warnings and passing messages. If blood was exchanged between a Pixie and a Witch, certain stipulations expressed, and a secret told, the Pixie could not reveal the secret unless the terms of the oath were fulfilled."

"Couldn't or wouldn't?" I asked.

"Could not. It is called a geas. You have heard the expression 'his tongue was tied'?" I nodded and she continued, "We are not physically able to speak the words of the secret unless the parameters of the contract are met. Our current keeper of the collective knowledge knows all the untold secrets of our hive whose terms have not been met through the years. She keeps them unless she can fulfill the agreement; if she cannot, they are passed to the next keeper, and if she can rid herself of the secret, it is wiped from the collective." Maybe they knew something about Lorelei, and no one had ever bothered to ask them. It was highly doubtful, but worth a shot.

"Do you know how to break the pika Curse?" I asked as I turned into the driveway.

Clementine took a breath as if to give me an answer, but then seemed to notice which house I was approaching. This caused her to stop midflight and study my features carefully. I could see the wheels turning in her tiny brain until a realization dawned.

"You are Lorelei's family!?" Her statement was a cross between an exclamation and a question.

"I am Lyric Thindrell, her great-granddaughter." She considered this for a moment with her head cocked to one side, brows knit in concentration, before coming to a seemingly important conclusion.

"And you have recently manifested your powers?" I had no idea if this was an educated guess, or if Pixies had some way of knowing these things. I realized they had known I was a Witch from the start without my having done anything to alert them to the fact.

"In January, right after my thirteenth birthday," I supplied.

"There is someone I think you should meet. I am not the current secret keeper, but I believe she would be interested in you," she declared, her tone showing a newfound respect. "Please, follow me to our hive, Lyric Thindrell, heir of the Mountain Caretaker."

The Pixies soared around the side of the house to the back, and I traipsed after them, fairly running to keep up. Under the deck, I noticed some windows and a sliding glass door, probably an outside entrance to Allegra's apartment. As we started down the steep embankment toward the stream, the decline was so sharp, I was worried I would not be able to keep my footing, but we stopped beside a towering old growth Engelmann spruce. The lower limbs were hanging down thickly all around to form a teepee-like structure at the base of the tree.

The Pixies glided under these spruce needled limbs, and I followed, finding myself in a fantasy world. The tree had teeny steps carved into the bark starting at the bottom, spiraling up and around the trunk several times before I lost sight of them in the foliage above. At intervals along the stairway and in some of the branches there were twig and bark houses complete with windows, doors, porches, roofs and even chimneys. They were expertly crafted with intricate details and soft yellow light spilling from many of the openings. I could tell the visible structures were just the outer part of a massive kingdom that lay tunneled inside chambers of the tree. The Pixies' wings emitted a soft glow of florescent light in the darkened atmosphere.

"Cormac," Clementine addressed one of the male Pixies, "please ask Cypress if she is well enough to come and speak to a guest for a moment. Tell her it is extremely important and might help ease her journey to the Beyond."

Moments later Cormac, assisted by two other male Pixies, half carried, half flew with a frail, ancient Pixie to a limb at my eye level.

"Cypress," said Clementine addressing the elder Pixie in a voice filled with deep reverence and respect, "This is Lyric Thindrell, the Caretaker's apprentice."

Turning to me she continued in a voice filled with formality, "Heir of the Mountain Caretaker, this is Cypress, keeper of our collective knowledge. She has memorized our whole oral history and is working to pass it on to our Pixie children, and to select a keeper to carry on our tradition. Cypress, Lyric's powers manifested this winter past, in her birth month, the one the humans have named January. She has some questions for you."

"Speak child, for I have not long on this earth and will soon begin my journey to the Beyond. Ask your questions," she commanded.

"Do you know how to break the pika Curse?" I asked again.

"No," she sighed in disappointment, considered me for a moment and then added "but, if we are asked, we will tell what we do know." This last was spoken forcefully, almost desperately, like she needed to let something out if only I would unlock the door. *Okay*, I thought, *so it's like a riddle.* She had given me as much of a hint as she could without breaking the blood oath. She obviously knew something. I just had to phrase the question correctly, not about the Curse exactly, but something related to it. I needed to change the hypothesis. If Lorelei hid the grimoire and her notes, maybe she gave the Pixies a clue as to where she had hidden them.

"What do you know about my great-grandmother, Lorelei's, last day on earth?"

Cypress beamed a toothless grin, and her whole countenance changed.

"Finnick Grey, Alaric Noble and Reverie Thindrell, in turn, have all asked us about the evil one's grimoire, Lorelei's notes, and the Curse, and in each generation, we have answered truthfully, we know nothing of these things, but no one, save you, has ever asked us what we know of Lorelei's last day. We were bound with a blood oath by Lorelei not to tell anyone but family this information because, on the day of her death, she was ill and suspected treachery, and did not know who her enemies were. You are family?" she asked in a ringing voice, gaining strength and momentum as she spoke.

"Yes," I answered clearly. I'm sure this was a formality of the blood oath since Clementine had already introduced me. Cypress bowed her head in relief at my affirmation and continued her narrative.

"The day Elowen was born, Lorelei went on two errands. When she returned, she came to us and bound us to secrecy. If, and only if, a family member asked where she had been that day, we were to tell them she had taken two gifts to her friends, one to Allegra and one to Briar." I didn't know Briar, but I was pretty sure if Allegra had Lorelei's notes or Jasper's grimoire, she would have given them to Reverie long ago, so I wasn't sure if this information was even relevant, but I could ask Allegra about it at tea tomorrow.

"We were given a gift of our own as a token of the bond. We were to return the gift to the person who released us from our oath."

"Will you show me this gift?" I inquired. Now we might be getting somewhere.

"Of course, Caretaker, it would be my ultimate pleasure." She smiled her gummy smile again.

Several Pixies were dispatched to retrieve the gift. Moments later, they dropped a flat, shiny metal bookmark into my open hands. From the feel and weight of it, I presumed it was pure silver. It measured approximately two inches by eight inches, and one side was polished so perfectly I could see my reflection clearly, but the other side, which contained line after line of small precise engravings, was tarnished so severely I couldn't decipher the inscriptions. I had no idea why this thing was important to Lorelei, or why she felt compelled to leave it in safekeeping with the Pixies.

"Caretaker?" Cypress asked cautiously. Only when I looked up from my examination of the bookmark and gave her my undivided attention did she continue to speak. "Now that the secret has been revealed, and the vow has been fulfilled, I feel I should confess some failings on the part of my predecessors before I go to my grave. I have lived 26 human years. This is 104 in Pixie years. When we keep a blood oath, someone must ask us a key question before the secret can be revealed. No one has asked this hive a question relating to Lorelei in two decades, which was before I became keeper."

"Go on," I encouraged. Maybe she could shed some light on the mysterious bookmark.

"Pixies like to collect shiny things, and I'm afraid some are quite greedy and vain." At this comment, I heard a few titters from the hovering crowd. "I fear Lorelei's secret was guarded too closely because the oath taker of the time, Callalili, was too proud and vain, and did not want to relinquish the mirror."

"Mirror?" I questioned and then realization dawned, "Oh, is that why the blank side is polished so brightly, this Callalili used it as a mirror?" Cypress and some of the others bowed their heads in shame.

"It was in deep violation of the spirit of the oath. Lorelei's oath had two parts. The *right* person had to ask the *right* question. If the wrong person asked the right question, or the right person asked the wrong question the geas overcomes us, and the oath literally binds our tongues. If parts of the oath are fulfilled, sometimes our tongues are loosed, and we can give hints, as happened with you, until our tongue is tied again, or the truth is revealed.

"When Finnick Grey, the family's lawyer, came to see Callalili, he was not a relative, so her oath kept her from telling him anything. Alaric Noble, Lorelei's spouse, came next. He was mourning a terrible loss, and I'm not sure what he asked when he came, because it was not recorded, and that fact is an unforgivable omission in our collective knowledge. However, I do know it was not exactly what Lorelei wanted her relative to ask, but Callalili's tongue loosed, meaning he was on the right track, and she could have given him hints to lead him into asking the right question, but she refused to help. She justified this behavior in her own mind by saying he was not a 'blood' relative, but Ric was Lorelei's husband, and she meant for him to have answers. This blood relative stipulation was not in the original contract with Lorelei, but Callalili had developed an unhealthy obsession with the mirror and had no intention of relinquishing it. She had an ornate frame made for it and hung it in her bedroom where she polished it every day.

"Have you ever played the game known as telephone where a group of children whisper a secret from one to another until it becomes so convoluted the last child ends up with a totally different message from the first child?" I admitted I had played the game at a birthday party when I was younger.

"Do you understand the dangers of an oral tradition? Any keeper can pass incorrect information if it benefits them, and no one will be the wiser. That is why I am trying to educate *all* our children in our oral traditions and secrets before I pass to the great Beyond. I think we need a system of checks and balances, so no Pixie becomes too corrupt or powerful.

"Callalili's successor was a Pixie called Ciara. Before she took her journey to the Beyond, Callalili passed on Lorelei's blood oath. She told Ciara only a blood relative could hear Lorelei's secret and part of the oath was to polish the mirror every day as she had been doing for years. Neither of these things were true, and she said them to cover her deceit, basically she lied to hide her own greed and vanity. Ciara told me she had often come upon Callalili talking to the mirror as she polished it.

"Elowen, Lorelei's own daughter, never sought us out, but Reverie came when she was seventeen to talk to Ciara. She was a relative, even a blood relative, but she never asked about the days before Lorelei's death, only about the Curse and the grimoire, and of those things, we have no collective knowledge.

"After many years, Ciara died, we moved the mirror to a more central location, so everyone in the hive could take a turn in the chore of keeping it polished. This January past on a winter's night, for no apparent reason it abruptly fell from its place, and the frame was broken beyond repair. On closer inspection, I discovered Callalili had placed a written confession between the back of the frame and the engraved side of the mirror telling everything I have related to you about her part in this deception."

Chapter 9

When I came in the front door, I shouted for Reverie, but only silence answered. I assumed she was not back yet. I buried the bookmark in my sock drawer. I didn't know what else to do until I got a chance to talk to Reverie. Since I would be doing my own laundry, I didn't think anyone would disturb it there. Then I retrieved the book, *Tools of Witchcraft,* from the attic and took it to my room, so I could read the chapter on candles. Somewhere between poring over purple candles being used for casting spells of wisdom, and green candles being used for spells having to do with luck or wealth, I must have drifted off to sleep.

The dinner chimes woke me. When I arrived at the table, there was only one place set and the food, spaghetti and meat balls, was already on my plate. The pikas were on the table gathered around my dinner. I think they wanted to keep me company. It was adorable in a freakishly odd way.

"How was your day?" asked my father, trying and failing to strike the right balance between concerned parent and friendly buddy.

"Let's see," I answered sarcastically as I sat, "I learned all my male relatives are rodents…"

"Lagomorphs, more specifically of the genus Ochotona," corrected Ric primly. I smiled; as an only child, it was fun to have someone to tease. I started eating.

"I met Elowen." I raised my eyebrows; someone owed me an explanation.

"Oops," Ric apologized. If you could have seen the sincerity of his expression, you would have realized that these were not animals, but people trapped in animal form.

"Yeah, oops is right." I glared. "A heads-up would have been nice."

"How is she?" asked Westley fondly, reminding me of a lovesick puppy.

"Scary as heck. She was having some kind of vision. She called me Cursebreaker," I remarked in confusion.

"She hasn't used that term in years," Ric mused and then noticed my panicked expression, "I wouldn't take it seriously if I were you. She used to call Reverie that all the time when Reverie was a teenager. Poor girl wasted so much time running around in circles trying to undo the Curse. She wanted so desperately to help her mother, and she knew breaking the Curse would go a long way towards bringing Elowen back from the brink. She finally came to terms with the fact that it would probably never be broken, not in her lifetime anyway. It's so sad, I know she would like to fall in love and get married, but she doesn't dare."

"Couldn't you find some other Witch to help Elowen? What about your parents, Westley? Surely your mom could train her. Elowen is her daughter-in-law, even if the situation is...er...somewhat unconventional."

"My parents died in a car wreck right before I met Elowen," he offered quietly.

"Oh, I'm sorry, I didn't know." I squirmed uncomfortably.

"Of course, you didn't, and it's okay. It was a long time ago. To answer your question, no, for a long time, we didn't know anyone else who could help Elowen. As pikas, we have no power. Witches are rare, and Elowen's powers are even rarer." Then he added softly, "You know, she can act and appear quite stable on most days, it's the visions... The visions seem to unhinge her. She can't control them. She doesn't get enough information to be of any use. I know it's just as frightening for her as it is for everyone else."

"Reverie helped her tremendously after she received her own training, and those Witches from the school helped, too, until the place shut down, and they all moved away to find other teaching positions," added Ric.

"It was Reverie who figured out Elowen would do better being away from others, except for Brownies and Pixies. For some reason, Elowen can't read the thoughts of the smaller Fae, and Brownies tend to have a soothing effect on others," chimed my father. He always seemed hesitant to join the conversations. I wondered if this was his nature or if his reluctance had something to do with feelings of unworthiness towards me, or guilt about not be able to be in my life.

"I visit her often," added Westley wistfully, "On her good days, we reminisce for hours about our courtship and honeymoon. Sometimes she asks about her daughters, and even about you." So, she knew about me. It seemed there were dozens of people who knew about me while I had never even been aware that they existed. It was a disconcerting thought to realize I had been kept in the dark all my life. It felt like a betrayal. Suddenly, I had another thought related to this afternoon.

"Where's Zeke?" I was beginning to think it strange I hadn't seen much of the Brownie at meals or around the house. I had gotten the impression earlier today Dara thought it was out of character for him, too.

"There was a big bachelorette party at one of Reverie's rentals last night. They checked out this afternoon but left a gigantic mess. A family reunion is checking in first thing tomorrow, so it's all Brownies on deck tonight to get the house shipshape in time," said Westley. It sounded reasonable; maybe I was overly suspicious.

"There is something else I think you should know," I began and told them all about my conversation with the Pixies. "So, Ric, do you remember what you asked Callalili about Lorelei?"

"No, it was 57 years ago, and I was so out of my mind with grief in those days I don't remember anything, much less a conversation with a random Pixie. I didn't purposefully seek her out to ask about a blood oath. I think I must have come upon her in the garden one day by accident.

"I didn't realize Lorelei had gone out the day Elowen was born," he clarified as he shrugged is little pika shoulders.

"For the first year that I was enchanted, I had to fight hard to overcome the natural instincts of the pikas. All three of us experienced this transition period when we were first cursed. Pikas don't hibernate in the winter, so they spend all summer collecting and drying grasses in order to survive the colder months in their burrows. Imagine my sorrow when I realized I had been running back and forth heaping dried plants in our basement, worrying about starvation and predators, literally wasting what little time I had left to spend with the love of my life, while she had struggled all hours of the day and night trying to crack this Curse as well as going through the fear and uncertainty of her first and only pregnancy virtually alone," he paused and I noticed a lump sliding down his throat as he blinked back a tiny tear.

"Can I see this bookmark?" he asked after taking a moment to collect himself. I sprinted to my room to retrieve it. When I returned, they all gathered in a small circle and studied the piece of flat silver intently.

"We need to get this inscription cleaned up," noted Vinn with some authority for the first time, "Zeke keeps the silver polish in the cupboard under the sink." I didn't ask how he knew this; I presumed as furry little creatures they knew all the nooks and crannies of the house and their contents. The directions said to wipe on a thin layer, wait five minutes and rinse. It worked like a charm; maybe it was charmed, who knew about Brownie cleaning products? Years of tarnish slid away. The engravings were not in English.

"Aztec or Egyptian?" asked Ric, deferring to Vinn who appeared to be the expert in languages.

"No, this looks like ancient Greek," observed my father as he peered closely, whiskers twitching. His little pink nose was so close to the text that I suspected he might be a bit nearsighted. I suppose it would be next to impossible to get pika sized eyeglasses.

"Yes!" exclaimed Ric. "Numbers, if I'm not mistaken. There should be a book here somewhere, with a chart inside. If you can locate the book, you could decipher the engravings."

"If this effected Callalili the way the Pixies described, it might be enchanted. I would say she got the largest dose because she handled it the longest. Pixies are extremely susceptible to Witch curses, partly because of their size, but I think we should take precautions just to be safe," cautioned Vinn.

"Let's put it in a clear plastic sandwich baggie, that way we can still see the inscription, but we won't over handle it. The baggies are in the top drawer by the dishwasher," advised Westley. I went to retrieve one and found them exactly where he said they would be. I slipped the bookmark inside and sealed it shut. "And, I think you should continue to keep it hidden until we know more."

"Yes, and..." Ric continued in a sagely, persuasive voice, casting me an appealing glance, "Do we all agree to keep this between us for now? Reverie has enough to worry about with her work." We heard the doorknob rattle at the front entrance, and I made a split-second decision for good or ill. I bolted to the back of the kitchen, through the hallway into the library and up the spiral staircase to stash the bookmark in my sock drawer again. I quickly ran back the same way, stopping to flush the toilet in the downstairs bath on my way through the kitchen into the dining room. Reverie was giving the pikas an update on the injured Centaur girl and the new foal.

"Oh," I lied when I saw Reverie and gestured behind me, "I was in the bathroom, and I didn't hear you come in." I slid into my seat and nonchalantly resumed eating my cold spaghetti.

If she hadn't looked so rumpled and tired, she might have noticed the nervous glances I exchanged with the pikas, but I remembered she had been awake even before me this morning and hadn't had the luxury of an afternoon nap. Poor Reverie; she worked so hard to make everybody happy and to do her duty. She truly was compassionate and charitable, but I wondered if she ever wanted a vacation from her life.

"What's the silver cleaner doing on the counter?" she asked as she peered through the arched opening into the kitchen. Westley saw the look of panic in my eyes.

"I don't know," he offered smoothly, "Zeke must have left it out."

"How odd, but he has been acting out of character today," she mused thoughtfully as she walked over and replaced it under the sink. So, she had noticed something off about the Brownie's behavior; I wasn't imagining it.

"Well, it's been a very long day. I phoned Zeke earlier and told him I had already eaten at the stables with Indigo and Viktor, so I think I'll head to bed. Lyric, we need to get started bright and early in the morning, say 7:00? Is cereal for breakfast alright with you? Tomorrow is grocery day, and I'm afraid there isn't much else unless you want pancakes again."

I assured her my diet had consisted mostly of cold cereal before coming here, and I preferred it. After she left, I took my dishes to the sink, rinsed them out, and placed them in the dishwasher, then turned and pointed my finger accusingly at the pikas.

"Okay, guys you'd better know what you're talking about because it did not feel good to lie to her." Reverie was the first adult

I'd met who seemed genuinely interested in who I was as a person and how I felt.

"Trust us," requested Westley, as they all nodded solemnly, "I think we know Reverie pretty well. Let's do some research before we bring her into this. At the very least, let us do some snooping around to try and locate the book with the translation chart for Greek numbers."

I agreed reluctantly and then decided to retire to my own room, so I could finish my reading assignment before bed. I was more determined than ever to learn all I could about magic as rapidly as possible.

Chapter 10

Reverie and I were back in the attic lab right after breakfast the next morning.

"You have plenty of raw power, and yesterday, you demonstrated a good level of control for a beginner," she encouraged with a supportive smile. She appeared alert and refreshed this morning, dressed in her unofficial uniform of jeans and unadorned t-shirt. She was fresh-faced and ready to tackle a new day. Her shoes, I noticed, had already been discarded under the table.

"We'll continue to work on your control every day. The control exercises should also improve your stamina. They will help you build up your reserves, so you won't get worn out and have a headache every time you use magic. I've decided that instead of a making a focus object like a wand or staff, you'd be better served if we create devices you can use for defense rather than offense," concluded Reverie.

At this point in my training, this line of reasoning made sense to me. Until I had absolute control of my abilities, I would be more vulnerable to attacks. My encounter with Elowen yesterday had made that all too clear. I had frozen, not knowing how to act. Even though she was harmless, I hadn't known that, and unleashing raw power on her in a moment of fear might have been a devastating mistake, but if she had been dangerous, not acting at all could have proven just as disastrous.

"So, today, we are going to craft a talisman called a valerian trinket. It's a pendant filled with valerian root designed to protect the wearer against black magic. If that goes well, tomorrow we'll make a water charm." As she was talking, she bustled around the lab assembling various implements and ingredients. She laid a delicate necklace on the table. Attached to the chain by a small hoop was a circular gold locket about the size of a nickel. The two hinged sides were open, showing it was empty. A normal locket usually held small photographs of loved ones; however, the chambers of this model were deeper and slightly more spherical. The outside surface was unadorned.

"Now," she instructed, "an amulet already has natural power, but a talisman is charged with magic for a specific purpose. We are going to take this pendant, which has no magical ability, and cast a spell on it to make a talisman. According to your reading, which color candle do you think we should use to make the valerian trinket?"

"Hmmm, black, I think," I recalled with my head cocked as I concentrated on remembering last night's reading assignment. "Black is used for banishing and for protection, so if the talisman is supposed to protect against black magic, I think that should probably work."

"Excellent," she smiled broadly showing the slightest dimple in her rosy cheeks. I felt a warm glow at her praise. "Valerian is an herb with powerful magical properties; not only does it protect against black magic, but it can also enhance the power of a spell or ritual. The trinket will keep small evils away altogether and can be used in spells to banish greater evils, like Demons. It will be important for you to do most of the actual spell crafting since this will be for your protection, otherwise the spell will not be keyed to you."

Among her tomes, Reverie had an ancient, leather-bound volume called *The Book of Charms*. There were meticulously drawn diagrams on the ragged-edged, yellowing pages and precise instructions written in a curvaceously flowing script. I read step by step directions from the page labeled *Crafting a Valerian Trinket*. As we worked, she had me practice my telekinesis by gently floating the needed items she had lined up at one end of the table down the length of the table and into our waiting hands as they were required. Only once did she have to raise her hand suddenly and catch something just before it would have smacked me in the nose.

"Thanks," I breathed in relief. She didn't scold, just gave me a sharp look that belayed the need to stay focused.

We ground the valerian root in a mortar and pestle in a clockwise direction, poured it into the locket with a tiny silver spoon, drew a chalk circle on the floor, reinforced it with salt, and set four black candles around the circle using a compass to get the positions exactly correct. I understood now why there were no rugs on the floor in the attic. It was extremely important nothing impede the ability to make the protective circle.

Next, I had to carve a symbol of protection with a sharp metal stylus into the front of the soft golden surface of the locket. Reverie had me practice the image over and over with pencil and paper before I was allowed to touch the necklace. Because of my background in art, copying the symbol correctly was not the problem, but I had to shove just the most infinitesimal amount of power from my hand through the pencil and into the icon on the paper. The first paper burst into flames, but after about the tenth try, I got just the right amount without even scorching the paper, and the symbol glowed red for the briefest of seconds before fading to black. I let out a breath I had not realized I was holding. It was time to move on to the necklace.

"You only get one shot at this, so do it exactly as you just did," she cautioned, but nodded encouragingly. Mustering all my concentration and focus, I tapped my power and repeated the process on the locket with the tip of my tongue held between my teeth in concentration. It was perfect. I felt a tingle of energy rebound in my chest when the symbol flared red and slowly faded to black.

"Perfect," she praised, "you felt something, right?"

"Yes."

"That means you did the spell right. It's part of Newton's law."
She smiled broadly, showing her perfectly even white teeth. I felt
ecstatic.

"For every action there is an equal and opposite reaction?" I asked
in wonder. Finally, we had hit on something I understood. Mother
would be proud.

Next, using my power, she had me practice lighting the stub of a
candle not being used in the spell. Nothing happened, and after several
tries, I became frustrated.

"Relax," assured Reverie. "You're trying too hard. You've already
done it one. Close your eyes and imagine the paper you set on fire.
Now replace the image with the wick of the candle. Good."

When I opened my eyes, the candle was glowing warmly.

"Before we set up the final casting, let's practice the incantation.
It's in Latin, and your pronunciation must be perfect." She read it out
loud, and I repeated it until she was satisfied.

"Go ahead and step into the circle without disturbing the salt or
the chalk. Place the pendant on the floor in front of you." Next, she
taught me how to seal the circle with magic, so no foreign influences
could enter and alter the spell while it was being cast. Safety first. I
had to touch the salt and gradually feed power into it until I felt the
circle seal. The magic circle was not just a two-dimensional drawing
on the floor. I felt the energy rise around and above me like a half
spherical protective bubble.

"Okay," she smiled reassuringly. "Now, you are the only one who
can break the circle." To demonstrate she tried to reach out and touch
me, but her slim fingers pressed flat against an invisible barrier.

"This last part is crucial, when you speak the incantation, you
must let the magic know your intention. What do you need the spell
to do? Try to get a picture of it in your mind right now. Then, you
must have faith in the magic. Ready?"

"Yes?" Not really; I was scared, but I was good at imagining pictures, and I had an idea.

"Remember, believe in yourself. Believe in the magic. Light the candles with a bit of your will, and speak the incantation." I wiped my sweaty hands on my pants and gathered my power sending it toward the first candle. They all burst into flame at once. I laughed nervously.

"Ease off just a little," she admonished cautiously but with confidence.

I spoke the incantation, picturing myself clothed in a suit of shining armor, holding back darkness with a shield. The symbol I had etched on the locket became a bright white-hot glow, and this time, the rebound of power felt more like an electric shock. Startled, I gasped, then everything returned to normal.

"Great job! Now, break the circle by wiping away a portion with your foot, and put the necklace on," encouraged Reverie The talisman felt slightly warm against my skin and somehow comforting.

"You did well. Let's clean up and put everything away before lunch. Always keep a clean lab; it prevents instruments and ingredients from becoming cross-contaminated and losing their effectiveness. Spellcrafting is an exact science." She hummed a cheerful tune as she began to sweep the salt into a dustpan. I helped tuck away the spell book, bottle of valerian root, and candles. Then we washed away the remnants of the chalk circle, and scrubbed the silver spoon and the mortar and pestle in the farmhouse sink.

"I know you have tea with Allegra this afternoon, and I need to go into town to restock on groceries. I can get most of my spellcrafting supplies delivered to my front door using a mail order catalogue and the telephone, but no one will deliver groceries...or pizza. Nobody will bring pizza all this way," she sighed glumly with her perfectly arched brows knit in frustration. "What I wouldn't give for good pizza delivery."

"How far is it to the nearest grocery store?" I asked out of curiosity. I was used to having neighborhood convenience stores within walking distance of our apartment.

"Hmmm... In good weather? About a 15-minute drive. I usually buy several newspapers for myself and the pikas, so we can keep abreast of what is going on in the world. We are rather isolated here. Do you need anything while I'm out?" I shook my head slowly, trying to digest the fact that the pikas read the newspaper every week.

"Okay, for tomorrow, in *Tools of Witchcraft*, read the chapter on the uses of herbs and roots. We'll do lessons in the afternoon since I'll be going to church in the morning. Would you like to join me?"

"For church?" I asked in surprise. "Like some kind of Wicca ceremony?" Mother had never been religious, choosing to have faith in science rather than God.

"No, just regular church," she replied nonchalantly.

"Don't Christians have a problem with Witches, you know, the whole burning them at the stake philosophy and all?"

"That was hundreds of years ago," she chided. "Things have changed. All power comes from a central source, whether you choose to call that source the Universe, Mother Nature, the Mountain, God, Allah, Krishna, Buddha, or Jehovah, He is the same being. Everything good comes from the light, and everything evil comes from the darkness. Just because we have special powers, we're not evil. How we choose to use those gifts determines our nature. I believe in the Christian concept of a Divine Creator and practice their teachings. It gives me peace of mind, but you are free to follow your own conscience."

"Is it okay if I hang out with the pikas tomorrow instead?" I really wanted to get to know my father and other relatives, even if they were four-legged at the moment, and I hoped maybe we could make some progress on the bookmark.

"Yes, of course, I'm sure they would love to have your company."
She slipped her shoes on before heading downstairs.

After lunch, I decided to do my reading assignment in the attic,
so I could compare the descriptions in the chapter on herbs and roots
to Reverie's neatly labeled bottles, jars, and vials. At one point in my
wanderings, I stumbled upon a book about potion making and
couldn't resist pulling it out and peeking. It contained spells for hundreds of potions and counter-potions that could do almost anything.
I skimmed a few chapter headings: "Changing Your Appearance";
"Curing Illness"; "Energy – How to Boost or Drain"; "Invisibility –
Hiding in Plain Sight"; "Temporary Infatuation"; and "Poisons –
Sleep, Sickness, or Death." I got so wrapped up in reading, I almost
forgot about teatime with Allegra, but to my relief, when I remembered and glanced at the clock, I still had five minutes.

I stumbled into the foyer just as Reverie was leaving for the mar-
ket. She pointed to the door leading to the basement in the hallway
by the laundry room.

"Allegra's door is the one on the left at the bottom of the stairs."

I made a noise to let her know I understood and continued on
my way.

The staircase was completely enclosed, and at the bottom was a
hallway containing three doors, one on my right, one on my left, and
one down the hallway behind me. I knocked on the one on my left,
and Allegra answered and invited me in. She was dressed once again
in formal Victorian attire. Today her floor length gown was emerald
green and made of crushed velvet with white lacy trim. Her hair was
plaited in one long braid, and I must admit, I had hair envy.

The space was charming. Allegra lived in a walkout basement.
While three sides of Reverie's lowest floor were almost completely
underground, the fourth wall was at ground level with large windows

and a sliding glass door that opened to a terrace under the deck and showed a pleasant view of the wooded area behind the property. While the quarters were spacious, it was an efficiency apartment, meaning there were no walls to separate the bedroom, kitchenette, and living areas. Only the bathroom, which was tucked into a compartment beneath the stairs and had its own door.

"I have everything set up on the terrace," she said, leading me outside to a small bistro table set with a starched tablecloth and silver tea service. "It's such a nice day, I'd hate to stay indoors. I made peppermint tea; I hope you like it." She poured the tea and offered me an assortment of scrumptious looking iced petit fours.

"They sell baked goods in the deli at the resort," she volunteered in explanation. I think she was trying to be the consummate hostess by assuring me she hadn't gone to any trouble to obtain our refreshments. The shining tea set and impeccable linens told me otherwise.

"They look delicious, thank you." I chose one and stirred two lumps of sugar into my tea. The temperature was perfect on the terrace, and again I noticed the crisp, clean scent of growing things in the air and the explosion of green leaves and darker green needles on the various trees.

"It's so lovely. How long have you lived here?" I asked to make polite conversation.

"I came to the Mountain in 1943 after I escaped an internment camp in southern Utah for Japanese-American citizens. I'd been sent there from San Francisco after the Japanese bombed Pearl Harbor. Americans were very suspicious of persons with Japanese heritage in those days. I could have escaped earlier, or not have been captured for that matter, but I had friends..." Her voice died away at the memory. It was several seconds before she resumed, her voice taking on a false perkiness people tend to use when they are trying to cover up unpleasant emotions.

"The Mountain was a good place to hide at the time, and I liked it so well, I bought a house and stayed. About 10 years ago, Reverie renovated this house. She updated the bathrooms and kitchen upstairs and added this apartment and a nicer place for Zeke and the pikas downstairs. This was all unfinished basement before. I had already decided my house was too big for one person, so I sold it to her and moved in here."

"So, you knew my great-grandmother, Lorelei?" I asked, realizing she had provided the opening in the conversation I needed to introduce this topic without seeming rude.

"Yes," she said fondly, "Lorelei and I were the greatest of friends. We used to go on shopping trips together down to the valley. She loved to buy paintings and artwork."

"I understand she gave you something the day before she died?"

"Why, yes, would you like to see it?" If she wondered how I had gained this information she didn't let on. She led me back into the apartment and gestured to a painting on the wall over her bed. It was a rather gloomy, depressing landscape of a river flowing between a narrow, craggy mountain pass at night. I'm sure I looked as puzzled as I felt.

"The artist is quite famous. He is an American named Albert Pinkham Ryder, this was painted in the late nineteenth century, but I'm afraid it's only a reproduction. The original hangs in the Smithsonian Institute in Washington D.C. The setting is a real place. It's the site of many fatal shipwrecks," she offered.

There was nothing special about the painting; in fact, it was quite the opposite. I found it almost dismally repulsive. There was certainly no place to hide a grimoire or a notebook filled with translation notes. I was beginning to wonder if the Pixie, Callalili, had held back greater information than she shared in her written confession.

"It's all about death, isn't it? Why would she give *this* to you?" I asked in confusion.

"Occasionally, she went through dark periods after Jasper was killed. I think she partially blamed herself for his death because she was the one who lured him to the place on false pretenses. She led him to believe she had changed her mind about marrying Ric; afterwards, even though she knew Jasper had murdered and tortured numerous people and would continue to do so, she was riddled with guilt for her deception.

"Off and on, in the first years after he died, she collected art all having the same theme, but after she found she was going to have Elowen, she drastically changed, became much happier than she had ever been. To answer your question, maybe she wanted to be completely rid of this dark phase of her life, prepare to move on to her new role as a mother," then she added as an afterthought, "Mostly though, I think, I was the only one she knew who would appreciate the artwork."

"And there was nothing else?" I asked hopefully.

"No," she answered bewilderedly, "why do you ask?" So, as we went back to our tea, I sat and told her all about my experience with the Pixies. "How did she seem that day?" I asked as I finished my story.

She considered my question for several seconds before giving me a slow, thoughtful answer.

"A little sallow, anxious…cagey even, but when I found out she was already in labor when she visited me and had given birth that night, I chalked it up to that, especially after I found out there had been complications, and she had passed away."

"Did she say anything unusual before she left you that day?" I asked as I leaned forward in my chair, hoping for something concrete.

"She told me to keep the painting safe for her because she might have to leave after Elowen was born. Later, I wondered if she had a premonition of her own death."

"But, didn't you think it odd to be so concerned about a painting, especially if she thought she was going to die?"

She opened her mouth to respond, checked herself and closed her jaw firmly.

I knew some older people had superstitions about speaking ill of the dead. I looked at her imploringly, "You had a thought, tell me please, it might be helpful."

"Frankly child, I thought she was addled in the brain."

Chapter 11

Reverie left for church at 8:30 the next morning and promised to be home before 11:30. As soon as I heard her car drive away, I retrieved the bookmark and headed down to the pikas' lair. I already knew which door belonged to Allegra, so that left me with only two choices, one down the hall behind me and one to my right, which gave me a 50/50 chance of finding the pikas' place.

I turned and strode down the hall behind me and gazed through the open doorway. It was a cozy room. The two outside walls exhibited the original stacked stone foundation. The furniture was all the same shade of rich dark walnut as the wide plank hardwood floors. There was a pleasant fire in a small stone fireplace and just in front of the hearth on a well-worn rug sat a child's table with four pintsized chairs. The table was laid with a little china tea set as if there were a tea party planned in the nursery for later in the day. I noticed a neatly made bed of intricately carved wood in one corner, probably used as a toddler's bed in pioneer times, and in another corner, I saw a glass-fronted curio cabinet from the same period containing a collection of diminutive porcelain figurines.

"Lyric?" called Westley pleasantly as he peered around the door-frame at the opposite end of the hall, "I thought I heard someone come down the steps. We're down here." Reluctantly leaving my unfinished survey of Zeke's domain, I followed Westley into the pikas' realm.

Here, the walls had been finished with drywall, the floors were a polished concrete, and it was noticeably cooler. Three small transom windows located high on one wall let in some filtered light. The ground outside came to the bottom of the windowsills, telling me we were indeed underground. A decked-out dollhouse with white clapboard siding was pushed up against the wall under the windows. This was certainly no store-bought, pink, plastic affair. The house had ramps between each of three floors instead of stairs, providing easier access to the different levels for densely furred feet. One bedroom took up the top floor with the pitched roof overhead, two more were located side by side on the middle floor. All three contained a pillow big enough to be a pika-sized bed and a few scraps of flannel for bedding. The entire bottom floor was the pikas' bathroom, a luxury spa for Ochotona, with tiny tile from floor to ceiling. I had wondered why our pikas didn't have a musky animal smell; obviously, they took hygiene to the next level.

"And it all works, too," commented Ric as I stared with wide eyes. "Plumbing, running water, and electric lights. We have push button switches at our level, so we can operate everything easily."

Mounted about a foot off the ground on the wall next to the doll-house was a 20-inch flat screen television. On the floor under the television was a DVD player, a stack of DVDs, and an array of comfy cushions. I raised my eyebrows quizzically. This was the only electronic equipment I had seen in the house.

"It was Vinn's idea," said Westley when he saw my surprise. "Reverie rents the DVDs at the public library or sometimes if we like them a lot, she buys them for us. It keeps us up to date with current culture."

"Culture?" scoffed Vinn. "That's what he tells himself, but mostly he likes to watch *Rambo* and *Jason Bourne* and *Terminator*. I prefer dramas; sometimes Reverie rents a whole season of a popular television show, and we binge watch." I had to agree that while newspapers would be one way to keep up with the outside world, modern DVDs would give a whole new meaning to the term "current events." It was also a great way for them to pass the time on long winter evenings.

"Does Reverie watch with you sometimes?" Personally, I couldn't see neat and clean Reverie sprawled on the floor watching Rambo.

"Oh, she doesn't really enjoy the types of shows we do. She's more into romantic comedies, so she has her own television in her private sitting room upstairs, only she keeps her TV and DVD player in a cupboard behind closed doors. It's her one guilty pleasure," said Westley as he waggled his eyebrows at me. These people had been holding out on me! I had been known to indulge in some Netflix binging myself.

"Well, I'd love to come down and watch a movie with you sometime. I can recommend some really good choices," I remarked casually as if it wasn't a big deal, but in my head, I was chanting: Please, invite me! Please, invite me!

"Do you enjoy musicals?" asked Ric. "Nobody will watch them with me."

Behind Ric's back, Vinn rolled his eyes and Westley stuck his paw down his throat in a mock gagging gesture. With only a slight twitch of a smile, I assured him I would be honored to watch musicals with him. Okay, I know it's silly because it had only been two days since I had last used technology, but television, computers, smart tablets, and cell phones had been an integral part of my life, and something I had entirely taken for granted until I had arrived here. I was in the throes of severe technological withdrawal.

Sensing the need to change the subject before Ric launched into a discourse on his favorite musicals, Vinn gestured proudly to another wall, "Over here is our food supply."

Sitting side by side on a wide reinforced shelf spanning the length of the room were large sturdy wooden bins with hinged lids. Each one was carefully labeled: oats, dried corn, rice, barley, flax seed, and wheat kernels. Vinn scurried under a bin and pulled a lever causing a stream of oats to pour through a tube attached to a hole in the bottom of the bin and land in a trough underneath.

"Reverie fills the bins twice a year, and the rest of the time, we're pretty self-sufficient," bragged Westley. Yes, unless something happened to Reverie, but that was not an idea I wanted to think about. Being the Mountain Caretaker and family matriarch came with monumental responsibility, and Reverie seemed to be able to juggle all the balls and make it look effortless.

"It's a pretty cool set up," I marveled.

"Ric designed it, and Reverie had it built for us about 10 years ago," stated Vinn. I noticed all the walls in the room had zig-zagging little ramps up to the ceiling where tiny openings led to what I imagined were hidden passageways terminating under cupboards and behind bookcases in every part of the house.

The only other adornment in the room was a column about three feet tall on which sat the bronze bust of a distinguished looking fellow with Roman features sporting a laurel wreath on his head. The column was Doric in design with a round fluted shaft and simple, thick, substantial blocks for the base and cap. It was crafted out of an expensive wood, probably mahogany, rather than cement or plaster as might be expected. I stepped closer and noticed a heart-shaped metal plaque attached to the front face of the cap of the pillar on which the statue rested. The engraving on this title plate read: ALARIC.

"Is this supposed to be you?" I quizzed Ric with raised eyebrows.

"No, no," he chortled, "This is King Alaric of the Visigoths. He was the first conqueror of Rome in 395 AD. Lorelei bought him for me because she said I was the Alaric who conquered her heart."

"Aww, that's sweet," I sighed.

"After Reverie built this place for us, I had her bring it down here. It makes me feel close to Lorelei."

Yes, sweet...and sad at the same time, I thought.

"We found the book," announced Vinn triumphantly.

"The one with the chart identifying Greek numbers? It didn't take you very long." Obviously, these little creepers got around.

"It's in the library upstairs. It was filed right where it was supposed to be."

"Hmm…" I murmured as I idly traced the heart-shaped plaque with my finger. I noticed my bitten nails were certainly not as nice a Reverie's. "Seems a little too easy if this was supposed to be some big mysterious clue. Kind of feels like a wild goose chase." The plaque was loose. The metal heart was only attached to the column with one small brad above Alaric's name. Absently, I flicked my stubby fingernail at the pointed end of the heart and the plaque swung up for a brief second revealing a keyhole underneath.

"Did you see that?" I exclaimed excitedly.

"What?" asked Ric.

"There's a keyhole under the name plate." I knelt and ran my fingers over the front surface of the column's cap piece. There were no visible seams, but I had a hunch. The chunky, cuboid, top section of the plinth where the keyhole was located was at least four inches thick, plenty of room to support my hypothesis.

"I think there might be a hidden drawer in this section on the top of the column. Do you have the key?" All three of the small animals turned their faces upwards and squinted at the column, looking for evidence of my theory.

"No, I've never even seen a key. I don't see any indication of a drawer. I don't think Lorelei knew there was a secret compartment," then Ric added skeptically, "Well… That is, if there is one. No offence, dear."

"None taken," I shrugged. I think I was beginning to grasp at straws and see clues where no clues existed. *Relax*, I told myself, *it's important to stay objective. They've been trying to break this Curse for nearly six decades and you've been here for less than three days. Be reasonable!* However, there was no denying the keyhole. Keyholes meant keys, and keys opened doors or drawers or something, whether it was important was yet to be determined.

"I'm pretty sure she bought the statue and the column together with the plaque already attached and covering the keyhole, but I could be wrong," he added as a blatant attempt to make me feel better, "I'm finding there's a lot I didn't know about the last few months of her life."

"I think it might be a good time to head up to the library and check out that book," proposed Vinn in yet another attempt to ward off Ric's melancholy. I agreed, and they set off on their route, up the ramps attached to the walls, as I set out on mine, up the stairs. On my way out, I noticed Zeke's door was now firmly closed. Was it something I did, or was I just being paranoid? I got the feeling that Brownie really did not like me at all.

The pikas were already assembled when I arrived. Sheesh, they were fast little buggers. Vinn pointed out the location of the book, *Identifying Symbols in Ancient Languages,* and I snagged it and secured some paper and a pencil. We found the bookmark had numbers organized in groupings of two, and they were in Greek as Vinn had surmised, but they were arranged totally illogically. I acted as scribe as the pikas scurried between the bookmark and translation chart, double-checking then taking turns calling out the numbers. It took an exasperatingly excessive amount of time.

"43 dash 112 comma." *(Wait...wait...wait.)*

"89 dash." *(Wait...wait...wait.)*

"21 comma, it goes on and on," moaned Westley. "There are at least 50 pair." I wanted to whine with Westley but thought better of it. Sometimes I got the impression that his emotional maturity hadn't progressed much since the time of his Cursing.

"Closer to 75," theorized Vinn. We plodded along, number after number, the pikas often consulting one another and asking for clarification before continuing.

"224 dash." *(Wait...wait...wait.)*

"13 period," exclaimed Ric triumphantly after almost two hours. "That's the last one."

"It's a quarter past 11:00. We haven't got much time before Reverie returns. Any idea what it means?" I asked and received three negative responses. "Okay, brainstorm with me for some common uses for a series of numbers."

"Social security numbers, driver's license numbers," volunteered Westley. Those were numbers you could use to locate someone. I could tell he had been a private investigator in a former life.

"Bank routing numbers, phone numbers, or IP addresses," called out Vinn, who had a more modern perspective on things, having been a pika for the shortest amount of time.

"Yes, good ideas," I commented as I focused on our translation trying to make something fit. "But, none of those things are set up like these numbers. Here we have groupings of two numbers with dashes in between and each grouping is separated by a comma." Then I realized we had a huge fault in our logic.

"Remember, this is as old as Jasper Finch's original Curse, so I'm guessing it's not computer related, or anything remotely modern. I think we need to narrow our thinking to World War II or earlier," I suggested as I unconsciously tapped the pencil against my forehead. "That was about the time Lorelei and Ric got married and Jasper pronounced the Curse upon them."

"It might be a book cipher," surmised Ric as he pulled on his left ear, something I noticed he did when he was in deep thought. "Spies used them a long time ago to pass messages. The first number refers to a page in the book while the second number is the location of the word on the page. If both parties had a copy of the same book, they could pass these coded messages, but without the book that acted as the cipher's key, enemies could not translate the message if it accidently came into their hands."

We heard tires crunching on the gravel driveway. My heart leapt into my throat, and I felt the color rise in my cheeks. Fear, guilt, and deception were not nice emotions.

"I'll go put all this away. You guys keep her occupied until I get back." Between the unfinished meals and the adrenaline inspired sprinting I was doing, I wasn't going to gain any weight while I was here. I was extremely frustrated about reaching yet another dead end.

At some point before I'd gotten up that morning, Zeke had baked bread and placed ingredients for a hearty stew in the crockpot. Reverie and I enjoyed the food while seated at the bar in the kitchen. The pikas, who were herbivores, munched on a crust of bread and kept us company.

"I miss steak," commented Westley as he looked longingly at our stew.

"No, you don't," replied Ric derisively, "Our bodies don't even crave meat in this pika form. It would be like Lyric saying she missed eating dirt."

"I know," sighed Westley morosely. "But I miss the idea of missing steak."

Reverie snorted, and I giggled.

"Lyric, I need to go over to Finnick's house for a few minutes and sign some papers. Friday was the last day of the month, and he likes to go over the numbers with me at the end of each month. He wants to meet you, and I think there will be treats involved. Would you be interested in joining me?" asked Reverie.

I had never met a treat I didn't like.

* * *

Finnick's house was the large modern lodge across the lane, the one I had noticed when I arrived last Thursday. There was a steep drive, and I was huffing and puffing by the time we got to the top, but the view of our little part of the canyon from his front porch was phenomenal.

"You're not used to the altitude," commented Reverie when she observed my heavy breathing. "Don't worry; by the end of the summer your lungs will adjust."

The door had a doorknob at the traditional human height and an additional knob much lower. Did our door have a second knob? I hadn't noticed. Reverie rang the bell, and it made an impressive gonging sound. It was answered by a Brownie woman wearing a white bib apron over her tan linen dress and a white ruffled cap on her spiky hair. I deduced the apron and cap had been made from a linen dinner napkin because I recognized the embroidered border across the bottom from a set used at Reverie's table on Thursday night when we had dined with Allegra.

"Come in, come in," she sang. "Welcome Miss Reverie. Miss Lyric, I presume? I'm Tansy, another of Zeke's cousins. Mr. Finnick is waiting for you in the parlor."

"Probably had a stain on it they couldn't get out," whispered Reverie when she saw me eyeing the dinner napkin turned apron as Tansy ushered us into the parlor.

It was a handsome room with velvet drapes, an expensive oriental rug, furniture upholstered in burgundy leather, and a heavy, masculine, oak desk. Finnick Grey rose from behind the desk and came forward extending his hand. I don't know why I was expecting him to be a Warlock, but he was unquestionably not. At the hem of his impeccably tailored trousers protruded bushy hair and cloven goat hooves. His feet tapped loudly on the areas of the floor with exposed hardwood. He had a neatly trimmed goatee, pointy ears, and small horns sprouting from his curling brown hair. Most disconcertingly, his black pupils were horizontal slits within his round amber hued irises. Finnick Grey was a Faun, a half-man and half-goat, one of the immortal Fae. People around here sure had a way of keeping important information from me. Either they were afraid my psyche couldn't handle all the facts, or more than likely, they were so used to magical creatures, it never crossed their minds I might need advanced warning.

"Lyric," offered Reverie, "This is Mr. Finnick Grey, our family attorney and good friend. He oversees our estate, including booking reservations for my rental properties. His employees were invaluable in managing and maintaining the properties during the years my mom was missing."

"Lorelei was a good friend. After her untimely death and the abduction of Elowen, it was the least I could do. It's a pleasure to meet you, Lyric. How are you settling in?" he said warmly in a cultured British accent.

"Just fine, thank you." Again, I found myself hard pressed not to stare at his unusual features.

"Have a seat on the settee while Reverie and I go over a few business things. We'll join you in a moment. I think the Brownies have some refreshments prepared." As if on que, three Brownies, Tansy and two males, entered carrying a pitcher, a tray of glasses and a platter of cookies. They carefully arranged the items on the coffee table. Finnick and Reverie had their heads bowed over some papers on the desk, and I was eavesdropping.

"Good news," he was saying, "They accepted your cash offer to buy Aspen Bliss, and because it has six bedrooms, you should be able to get $10,000 a week to rent it out, $20,000 during the holidays. Congratulations, you now own 12 properties, all mortgage free! I just need to get one or two signatures from you to finalize the deal."

He offered her a pen and pointed to a place on a document.

Twenty thousand a week, for one rental? Of course, she occupied one of the houses, and she provided one for Elowen, which meant she could only rent 10 of the houses. Certainly not all of them could possibly be occupied every day of the year, and smaller houses would command smaller fees but still, with 10 vacation rentals, I'd bet she cleared over a million dollars a year. No wonder she could afford to keep a separate house for her mother and traipse around in the forest delivering potions and administering first aid to magical creatures. It had been stated several times that she made a nice income from the properties, but there was nice, and then there was *niiiiice!* I was so busy trying to do the math in my head, I hadn't noticed the Brownies all gathered around my knees, politely waiting to get my attention. Finally, I focused on them.

"Miss Lyric, these are my brothers, Felix and Jonah," said Tansy with a small curtsy.

"So happy to meet you," declared one of them, I wasn't sure which. The Brownies I had met so far were congenial, willing to please, and happy to help. They fairly doted on those they served. It seemed being friendly and welcoming was not only part of their natures, but a code by which they lived.

"Zeke is so lucky to have a young one at his house again," announced the other wistfully. The three of them practically swooned at the thought.

"Well, I have only spoken to Zeke once, on the morning after my arrival," I said, hoping to see what reaction it caused. Tansy seemed puzzled but schooled her features quickly, and the boys shook their heads in wonder. "I assume he is somewhat reserved and chooses to remain invisible around me?" I offered as a possible explanation for what seemed to be atypical behavior on the part of a house Brownie. Reverie had told me that Brownies used invisibility as a glamour.

"No, Miss Lyric," fretted Tansy as she shook her head. "Zeke cannot be invisible in the presence of a Witch. It's not possible."

Chapter 12

Finnick and Reverie picked that moment to join us, and the Brownies silently retreated before I could ask any more questions. He poured me a glass of lemonade and offered me a cookie then turned to Reverie, "Your properties did really well in May. I'd say it was above average occupancy, especially for the off-season, and all 10 rentals are booked starting today through Labor Day weekend, and because of demand this year, you'll be charging almost as much as you do during ski season."

Reverie smiled demurely and accepted her own lemonade and cookie. It was evident that all this talk of money in my presence was making her uncomfortable, but Finnick, on the other hand, seemed to thrive on it. I could almost picture him rubbing his hands together in glee as he counted his golden coins.

"How long have you been practicing estate law, Mr. Grey?" I asked trying to change the subject to alleviate Reverie's discomfort.

"Since 1829." I choked on my lemonade and coughed uncontrollably for several seconds.

"So sorry," he replied after I could breathe again, "I forgot your limited experience with our world."

"How is it you manage not to attract suspicion amongst the human population?" I croaked after I had recovered enough to be able to talk. From my reading, I had learned the Faerie queens were not keen on their subjects drawing too much human attention. They preferred to live anonymously, which not only afforded them relative peace, but the occasional opportunity for mischievousness and trickery in our world without being suspect.

"I crossed the Atlantic in a ship from the British Isles in 1850. The Fae cannot teleport across water," he added by way of explanation. "I worked in New York City for a while before coming west and setting up a practice in town. I allow my glamour to naturally age at the rate of an average human. Every 40 years or so, I pretend my favorite great-nephew from Britain, my namesake, of course, is coming to take over my practice, so I can retire. I arrange all the paperwork for him to inherit the business, and then I suddenly fall ill. He, or in reality, a younger version of me, arrives and steps in, and life goes on with no one the wiser."

"Very clever," I acknowledged. Almost by accident, I discovered if I tapped the tiniest tendril of my power and cast a glance at him, I could see his glamour. To the outside world, he appeared as a clean-cut middle-aged man in an expensively tailored three-piece suit.

He shrugged.

"It's been a nice diversion from the drudgery of life in the Faerie Kingdoms. While most Fae quite enjoy their lives there, I was never satisfied. Someday, I might return to the Everafter, but for now, I thoroughly enjoy the dangers of the human world." I cocked an eyebrow at the word danger. Why would anyone purposefully choose danger?

Seeing my consternation, he went on to explain, "The Faerie Kingdoms are blissfully dull. There is no sickness, pain, or death, but there is also no personal growth. Everything your heart desires is provided for you. It is impossible to feel true joy if you have never experienced sorrow. In this world, not only do I have adversity and daily challenges, but I feel needed and have purpose. It's invigorating and never boring. There is also the thrilling possibility I could be stabbed or poisoned or shot dead and pass on to another realm, one most Fae never experience."

It was hard to believe he might be wishing for an unpleasant death, but day after day of sameness for millennia might be enough to make him desperate.

We chatted for another half hour before returning home. We found the pikas with the newspaper spread out all over the living room floor.

"You mother called while you were out," reported Vinn with a wince in my direction, "I told her you had found out about us." By us, he meant the pikas.

"What did she say?" I asked defensively crossing my arms.

"She said you could call her back if you wanted to talk about it," he held his paws out palms up in a gesture of peace.

"I don't," I declared as I glared at everyone in anger.

Reverie decided to save the water charm lesson for the morning when I wasn't so upset, which was a good idea since my mind kept wandering endlessly between Allegra's strange depressing painting, my lying Mother, a missing key, greedy immortal Fae, cipher codes, and an absentee Brownie. Since we weren't having a magic lesson, Ric asked if I would like to take a walk with him instead. Curious as to how the little pika would keep up with my much longer stride, I agreed. In the foyer, he suggested I place him on my shoulder, so he could converse with me easily, keep up, and be hidden from predators.

He instructed me to turn left out of the driveway and to take a road that forked to the right just past Finnick's driveway. There was a sign with an arrow pointing up the road labeled Riverwynd Stables. The street was steep, so I took my time. I could smell the horses corralled in a little dell about 50 feet off the road well before we reached them. We could see the new foal nursing from his mother, but we didn't see the Centaurs, so Ric encouraged me to press on. The paved street ended after we passed the stables and became a dirt road, which then narrowed further into a hiking path.

"They use these trails for cross-country skiing in the winter and horseback riding in the summer," Ric warned, "so, watch for manure piles."

"Thanks for the heads up, or maybe I'd do better to keep my head down in this case," I giggled at my own wit.

We continued up the rocky trail through dense mountain foliage scattered with wildflowers just beginning to bloom, purple phlox, and crimson Indian paintbrush among stands of gorgeous mountain fern. Presently, the trail opened into a huge, slightly sloping mountain meadow dotted with boulders. As we entered the meadow, I saw several wild pikas who had been sunning themselves on the large rocks, dive for their burrows cleverly hidden behind clumps of long grass.

"Can you communicate with them?" I asked in fascination.

"They have a language that consists of squeaks and a bleating high-pitched danger call, but mostly we speak using a sort of instinctual mental telepathy. The colony were very helpful to me when I first became a pika. They are like my extended family now." He paused and then pointed. "See that large boulder over there about two-thirds of the way across the field? Can you take me there?"

As I drew near, I noticed one side of the rock had a sheered face and an inscription was etched into the surface. It read:

Lorelei Killian Noble
Beloved wife and mother
1924-1962

"She used to bring me here, so I could learn from the wild pikas. She loved the meadow. That's why I put her remains here. The pika colony watch over her for me." Snow white columbine grew in clusters all over the grave.

It was a beautiful place, ringed by forest with mountain peaks towering all around. We stayed for a long time, not really talking, just lying back in the grass and watching the aspen leaves quaking in the breeze against their white bark, and staring at the dazzlingly blue sky above, allowing the quiet and calm of the place to penetrate our souls. It was what I had needed, and Ric had known. In that moment, I knew he loved me unconditionally, and I didn't have to do anything to deserve his love. It was a very peaceful feeling.

"Ric?" I asked uncertainly as we headed back home for dinner.

"Hmmm?"

"Tell me about my father. What is he like?" I realized Ric, and maybe Westley, had spent more time with Vinn than anyone else I knew, including Mother.

"He's an honest soul, and he loves your mother and you very much. He spends hours every year pouring over catalogues looking for the perfect gifts for your birthday and Christmas." I tried to think back on some of the gifts I thought had come from Reverie. Besides the poster of the asteroids, had there been books, maybe a telescope? I wished I had paid more attention, but little kids seldom do.

When we arrived home, I found Reverie seated at the breakfast bar while the infamous Zeke stood on a stepstool in front of the stove preparing quesadillas. I could only assume his manifestation meant he had received a stern lecture from his relatives for his dereliction of duties towards me. I was discovering that Brownies had a vast gossip network. Ric scurried away to join the other pikas in their domain.

"Hello, Zeke," I said with pointed cheerfulness as he peered at me sheepishly.

"Oh," replied Reverie with brows knit in confusion as she stared from me to him trying to work out the hidden meaning behind our words and cryptic body language.

"Hello, Miss Lyric," replied the Brownie quietly. He was obviously uncomfortable, and I interpreted it to mean something about me, or something I had discovered was deeply disturbing to him. I realized it was Zeke and Dr. Vinn Everton, my father, who had been conversing in hushed whispers under my bed on my first night in Reverie's house when I thought I had been dreaming. His voice had been confident and merry at that time. What had happened the next day to change his attitude toward me? Had my show of raw power during my first lesson with Reverie somehow unnerved him? I wished I knew more about Brownie magic and what made them tick.

"Dinner is ready, Miss Reverie." Zeke placed the plate of quesadillas on the bar where he had previously put our place settings, a pitcher of water, and a green salad. There were also little bowls of sour cream, fresh guacamole, and salsa. When I shifted my focus from the food, I realized Zeke had already left the kitchen.

"We usually eat our bigger meal at lunchtime on Sunday," said Reverie.

After dinner, I needed to be alone to think, so I told Reverie I wanted to read up on water charms before our lesson tomorrow. Without my own television or access to the internet, I found I had numerous hours for reading and contemplation.

When I got to my room, I paced and mulled things over for a very long time, trying to make pieces of illogical information fit into some sort of logical order. Something about Finnick Grey bothered me. He seemed a little too gleeful about the amount of money Reverie made, and hadn't the Pixie said he had come to ask about Lorelei's blood oath? Was he really a good friend trying to help, or did he have ulterior motives? I had read a lot lately about the how the Fae could not be trusted. What about Zeke? He was definitely acting funny. I did a mental shrug and decided to focus on something else.

I pulled the silver bookmark and sheet of transcription notes from their hiding place. I crawled into the massive canopy bed and closed the bed curtains, partially to block out distraction, and because I had always wanted a canopy bed with curtains that closed. I only had a twin bed at home. This bed made me feel like a princess in a fairy tale, but I had discovered in the last few days that fairy tales were not tales at all, and that information was still unsettling.

I forced my mind to concentrate on the bookmark. If Ric was correct, we needed a specific book to decode the numbers on the bookmark. I groaned in frustration. There had to be a billion books in the world. How were we ever going to know which one to use? *Think, Lyric,* I admonished myself. Could I narrow it down? Well, if it had something to do with the Curse, it had to be a book published before Alaric and Lorelei got married in 1946. Also, it was highly probable the book had significance to Jasper, but without his grimoire, it was impossible to determine what was meaningful to him. It was fruitless, circular logic. I groaned again, and decided to take a shower, read about water charms and go to bed.

* * *

The cereal was already out on the counter when I arrived in the kitchen the next morning, so I helped myself. Reverie came rushing in the side door as I held the bowl to my lips and drank the last of my milk.

"Insufferable Troll," she murmured as she closed the door looking disheveled and annoyed. "I had to walk all the way back up the hill to get a loaf of Zeke's leftover bread as tribute before he would call Blythe for me."

"Who's Blythe?"

"She's the Water Naiad who controls our section of the stream," she answered as she pulled a tiny vial of water from her pocket and held it out for me to inspect. "I felt I should ask for her permission before I collected the specimen, since we will be using it in a spell. The charm will be more effective if we use local water from a natural source. Our tap water comes from the stream, but it has been filtered, so it's not as potent. If you're ready, we can go up and get started.

"So, tell me what you learned about water charms?" she asked when we arrived in the attic.

"It's a vial of water enchanted to glow in the presence of magic, but it can also track the leftover traces of a Witch's spell."

"Correct. I chose this spell not only because I think it can be of use to you, but it's a completely different sort of spell from the one you did on Saturday." She placed the water filled vial on our work-table. It was a glass tube, about an inch and a half long and only a few millimeters wide with a cork stopper at each end. Reverie brought out a spool of thin wire, scissors, a jewelry making tool used to cut and shape wire, and some colorful skeins of embroidery floss.

"Ever made a friendship bracelet?" she asked as she kicked her flipflops under the table.

"Yes, last year at summer camp," I supplied in puzzlement.

"This will be similar," she instructed as she retrieved the chalk and the salt we used on Saturday. "Draw the circle around the table, so we can work within it, then reinforce it with salt as we did before. Step inside before you close the circle with your will." She surveyed the table to make sure everything was in place before she sat down. Once I sealed the circle, we would not be able to leave the table until the spell was complete, or risk ruining it.

Reverie snipped two small pieces of jewelry wire and inserted them gently into the corks at the ends of the vial. She had me choose my three favorite colors of embroidery floss and lay a long strand from each skein on the table. She tied them tightly to one of the wires and bent and twisted the end of it so the floss could not escape. Taking floss of her own, she demonstrated a complicated knot. I practiced on her floss until I became confident I could do it on my own.

"You'll repeat the knot over and over, each time you do, you must push a little of your magic into it and repeat the incantation 'Ostende mihi magicus.'"

"*Ostende mihi magicus*," I practiced. "What does it mean?"

"Roughly translated: Show me the magic. Your pronunciation is perfect, go ahead with the spell."

I fell into a rhythm as I felt the little rebound of tingling power with every knot I completed. When she decided the braided strand was long enough, she looped it over my wrist, so the vial was on top, and tied the end of the floss to the other wire, snipped it and secured it.

"Now, for a test," she declared. I broke the circle, and she stepped to the far end of the room and conjured her witchlight. The vial at my wrist glowed in a soft phosphorescent lime green.

Chapter 13

"Why do you think Mother never told me any of this?" I asked Reverie at lunch.

"About magic?

"Magic, my father, you… All of it," I replied sullenly.

"Aww, honey, it's complicated," she offered sympathetically. I gave her a baleful glance, and she tried again. "I imagine there are several reasons. I think she thought, or least hoped, you would be like her, not very powerful, so you could choose to lead a normal life, away from all this. What would be the use of filling your head with tales of magic when you had to live a non-magical existence? You couldn't tell your friends about it, could you? They'd think you were crazy, or a liar."

"She didn't really have to worry about that. I don't have a lot of friends." Reverie tilted her heart-shaped face and thought about it. She decided to use a different tactic.

"She raised you to be scientific in your approach to life. Yes?" I agreed. "Without seeing it with your own eyes, would you have believed it or thought she was having a break with reality?"

"Okay, okay, but keeping my father's existence from me?" I huffed with indignation.

"Lyric," she said slightly exasperated. "I know you're a smart girl and advanced for your years, but, and don't take this the wrong way, you *are* still a child, and your mother wanted to protect you as long as she could."

"Protect me from who? You, Elowen, my own father?" I snarled angrily.

"You must not judge your mother. She is doing the best she can. She and I experienced some real emotional pain while we were growing up. Our mother was an absentee parent most of our lives, our father wasn't really able to be a father because of his physical limitations, and thanks to that wonderful thing called sibling rivalry, Demelza was always jealous of me. Our community made her feel inadequate because she wasn't good at magic. She wanted to get as far away from here as she could and forget her past. She is driven to achieve recognition and find a cure for the Curse by using her own strengths. She wants to feel like she is good at something."

"Honestly," I sulked, "she's been almost as absentee with me as Elowen was with you."

"History has a tendency to repeat itself. We do what we know, often without realizing we're caught in a trap. We continue to make the same mistakes, generation after generation, until someone has the courage to break the cycle. Demelza never had a proper mother to be a role model, so she slips unconsciously into familiar behavior."

"You seem to be doing alright." I was beginning to feel more empathy towards Mother, but I was not willing to let my anger go just yet.

"I don't have a child, do I? Maybe I'm as messed up on the inside as she is. Adults are just children in grown-up bodies." I felt shocked by this revelation. Adults had all the answers, didn't they?

After our meal, I started down the hill for my pottery lesson. At lunch, Zeke had quietly served us. Reverie kept casting concerned glances at him. As I walked past the track to Elowen's house, she materialized from behind a tree and fell into step beside me. I tried not to show how much these sudden appearances of hers unsettled me. Today she was appropriately groomed and dressed in a denim skirt, red peasant blouse, and sandals. She didn't look much older than Mother. Most importantly, her eyes were normal.

"Cursebreaker?" she implored me softly.

"My name is Lyric, I'm your granddaughter," I replied, letting my annoyance show.

"Yes, of course, Cursebreaker Lyric?" she altered the title and asked for my attention again. I sighed, deciding to humor her.

"Yes, how may I help you, Grandmother?"

"I received a vision where I felt especially inspired to inform you that Elowen is a Cornish name which means Elm Tree."

"That is very interesting, Grandmother," I said, as if I were speaking to a preschooler.

"Do not patronize, granddaughter, this is extremely important," she stated quietly before once again locking eyes with me in a powerful soul gaze for a brief second. Abruptly, she stopped walking, turned in a circle, just as Reverie had done in *The Art Hut* on Friday, and disappeared. This time, I was certain there was a puff of smoke.

"Oh, for pity's sake," I grumbled, "Don't I have enough to deal with without adding a mentally unstable grandmother to the list?" I played an imaginary conversation in my head.

"Lyric, tell us about your family?"

"Well, my mother is a workaholic non-practicing Witch, and my father is a Warlock who has been enchanted to resemble a rodent-like creature."

I heard Ric chiding me, even though I'd said rodent-like instead of rodent, and I felt the corners of my lips switch in a smile. Whoever heard of a pika anyway? I harrumphed. For the hundredth time, I wished I had internet access, so I could do some fact checking. If there were American pika, were there other types of pika, too? When I arrived at *The Art Hut*, Allegra asked how the magic lessons were progressing.

"Good," I commented automatically and then I realized they were going well, and it made me feel happy and confident, maybe for the first time in my life.

There were two other ladies in Allegra's class, a 30-something year old who lived in Lehi, which I thought I remembered passing on our way from the airport, and her mother visiting from Florida. I enjoyed the class and forgot about curses and strange family members for two hours. When we finished, I noticed Briar wrapping finished bars of soap in her studio. As Allegra was taking payment from the ladies and explaining the need to come back later in the week to get their fired pieces, I slipped over and knocked on the glass. She glanced up and smiled shyly and beckoned me to enter.

Her skin was green, and her long wavy hair was the color of acorn hulls. She wore a crown of oak leaves and was clothed in a dress made of the same foliage. When I pulled on my power and looked at her glamour, I saw a pretty brunette dressed in a green t-shirt and bib overalls.

"You must be Lyric," she said quietly.

"Yes, I wanted to stop by and tell you how much I enjoy your soap." I was hoping to establish a rapport with her, so I could ask about Lorelei.

"Thank you, that's very kind." She continued wrapping the soap but didn't make any other comment.

"I only have Rosemary Mint." I stammered awkwardly attempting to lengthen the conversation. "Do you make other kinds?"

"Oh, yes, Basil Sage, Lemongrass, Goat's Milk, something I call Woodsman, that's very popular with the gentlemen, and many others depending on the season." She seemed to be warming up to me, or maybe she was just passionate about soap. I did a mental shoulder shrug and decided to barrel ahead.

"I understand you were friends with my great-grandmother, Lorelei, and she gave you something the day before she died? I was wondering if I could look at it. Do you keep it in your tree?" I asked.

She made a soft tinkling sound like windchimes as she laughed.

"The only thing I can put in my tree, little Witch, is myself. It is a healthy tree. You cannot place objects inside of it."

Oops, I had meant to read up on Dryads; at least she wasn't offended at my ignorance.

"But her gift is here, the bonsai tree, a Chinese elm." She gestured towards the plant on the drain board.

"Elowen means elm tree," I murmured out loud.

"Why, yes," she seemed surprised that I knew this, and for the first time turned her full attention towards me. "We gave it to Lorelei when we found out the baby was to be named Elowen. There was a party. All her friends from the Mountain attended, and the custom was to bring a gift for the baby. Humans call it a baby shower," she frowned and added in a puzzled voice, "But not like a rain shower."

I held back a bark of laughter at the look of confusion on her face, knowing it would hurt her feelings.

"Yes, I know the custom."

"Heath Tram made the blown glass bowl. It has small holes in the bottom, so the soil can drain when I water the bonsai. His wife, Poloma, made the silver sculpture of interlocking branches to hold the blown glass. The tree itself was my gift. I planted it in the vessel, showed Lorelei how to prune it and take care of it. It was a little elm tree for a little Elowen. We all thought it was a very clever play on words. Lorelei was delighted, but the day she died, she returned it and asked me to take care of it, and keep it safe for her and Elowen." She flushed deeply and hung her head.

"Briar, what's wrong?" She was obviously distraught.

"I could not return the gift. Lorelei died. I was supposed to give it to Elowen, but she was not here. I tried to give it back the day after she returned to the Mountain, but she was not interested in the little elm. She wailed like a Banshee, and told me to take it away," she exclaimed agitatedly. "I was afraid of her, but I should have insisted. I should have explained that it was a gift from her mother. It was what Lorelei wanted, but I thought Elowen would neglect the tree, and it would die. I had nourished it for so many years, I could not bear the thought, and so I kept it. I betrayed my friend. I was wrong. I am sorry."

By the end of her narrative, thick, sticky, sap-like tears were oozing down her green cheeks. I put my arm arms around her. Was it appropriate to hug a tree? Well, the environmentalists seemed to think so. Anyway, it felt like the right thing to do.

"Hush, now, it will be alright. Elowen can be frightening, and I think she was in a very bad place on the day after her return. She probably would have let the bonsai die, which would have been a shame. She could barely take care of herself, much less anything else. You did the right thing," I assured, and I patted her gently.

Confronting feelings and raw emotions was tricky, and I had always tried my hardest to avoid both situations. Mother and I were not huggers, and it made me uncomfortable to give such a physical display of consolation, but it seemed to help Briar pull herself together.

"Do you think so? No one ever asked about the tree before today. No one seemed to care if I had it, but I still felt guilty." She wiped her eyes with the back of her hand and sniffed. This was important. I had once again stumbled into an unknown fact.

"How did Lorelei act when she brought the bonsai to you?"

"Feverish, frenzied. I was worried about her," she said with concern. Both Allegra and now Briar had noticed Lorelei acting out of character on her last day, both mentally and physically. Had it been because she delivered a baby 12 hours later, or was there something else? Cypress, the elderly Pixie, said Lorelei had suspected treachery, and Ric had told me the birth itself had not been complicated.

"May I look at the tree?" She nodded and hiccoughed. Maybe I shouldn't have dismissed Grandma Elowen as crazy after all. Well, that was still a *big* maybe.

I went to the drain board and gently turned the tree in an unhurried circle. Bonsai is a Japanese art form literally meaning tray planting. It uses ancient cultivation techniques to yield small trees which mimic the shape and scale of full-sized trees. It was a beautiful tree with a lovely silhouette, painstakingly cared for, but in my slow survey, nothing jumped out. I rotated the plant again; this time I shifted my focus and concentrated on the complicated design of curling, interlocking branches Poloma had sculpted from molten silver. The room felt a little brighter. I glanced out the window, had the sun come out from behind the clouds? No, there were no clouds, only the usual vast expanse of cobalt blue sky. Slowly, realization dawned and in a measured, deliberate motion, I turned my wrist. The water charm was glowing a radioactive neon green.

It took me a heartbeat to recognize what I was looking at because it was so discreetly concealed, but then my pulse began to hammer in my ears, and my stomach flip-flopped. The color, thickness, and intricate curlicues of the hidden object, blended seamlessly with the design of Poloma's sculpture. Lorelei had used a spell to twist several of the branches to hold a small, old-fashioned, skeleton key.

Chapter 14

Freeing the key was like solving one of those brainteaser puzzles with twisted scraps of metal which must be manipulated in just the right sequence to separate the pieces. I had to lift the bit upwards, that's part of the key you slide into the lock, then pull the shaft towards me, and rotate the bow twice around the loop of a branch to dislodge it.

Briar had ventured closer as she observed my inspection of the plant and now peered earnestly over my shoulder.

"Has that key always been there?" she asked in awed wonder. "I'll swear to you, I never noticed. It was so cleverly concealed, wasn't it? It looks like part of the original design."

"I think a portion of Lorelei's spell was an illusion to make it blend in," I replied. "Can I take the key?" I felt a sudden anxiety to get it home as fast as possible.

"Of course, you are the Caretaker's apprentice, you can take whatever you want, the tree, the bowl, the sculpture. They all rightfully belong to you now anyway," she humbly offered.

"No, Briar, I want you to keep the bonsai. I have no need for it. Lorelei entrusted you with it, and you have done an honorable job of keeping it safe for her, just as she asked. She wanted you to have it. I only need the key. It's very important." Her shoulders, which had been slumped, straightened as she relaxed. Apparently, I had said the right thing.

"Thank you, but I cannot help but think the knowledge of this key might have saved much pain and heartache if it had been brought to the forefront years ago," she offered sagely.

"You are probably right, but we can't dwell on it now. The past is past. I really need to go." By this time, my restlessness had peaked and was almost palpable. My need to get home with the key overwhelmed me, so I sprinted out of the shop, past a stunned Allegra, and attempted to make the jaunt up the hill as fast as humanly—or Witchingly—possible. I ran clutching the key in my fist.

Eventually, I had to slow because of the physical exertion of the upward climb. Blasted altitude. As I passed the Riverwynd Spa, someone appeared in my peripheral vision a few yards to my right. I turned to face the apparition, and thinking it was my grandmother again, I opened my mouth to protest her startling appearances, and express my need to hurry, but this was not Elowen; not even close.

At first, I thought it was a rabid dog, but then it reared up on two legs. The being had a hollowed-out, emaciated humanoid form. The skin of a dead coyote was perched on his head, the lifeless animal's snout resting on the creature's forehead with the front paws draped over his shoulders, and the rest of the carcass falling down his back in a mess of matted fur. Filthy pelts of other animals hung around his waist as his only clothing. His fingernails and toenails had been filed into long razor-sharp claws. He had black lips, and his teeth were pointy fangs. His yellow eyes gleamed in his sallow face with a gaze of pure unadulterated evil.

One instant, he was a dozen feet in front of me, and the next, he was standing within striking distance. He raised a skeletal hand, and a putrid smell of rotting flesh overwhelmed me as he reached for the key. I was paralyzed with fear. This was the most vile, malevolent creature I had ever encountered. He was going to take the key and probably kill me. Ric, Westley, and my father would remain pikas forever, and no one would ever know what I had discovered.

Abruptly, a small red fox came streaking out of the woods and took up a position in front of me facing the apparition and snarling with teeth bared. The evil being hesitated, threw his head back, and produced a series of high-pitched, ear-piercing yips and barks. A dozen screaming howls answered his cries from deep within the woods, startling me and causing my adrenaline to spike. Without warning, he took a lightening swift swipe at the fox with those deadly claws.

"The talisman. Use the talisman!" came Allegra's voice from the mouth of the fox as she disappeared and reappeared behind the monster. He whirled in confusion diverting his attention from me.

I reached inside my shirt with my free hand and pulled out the valerian trinket, thrusting it nervously towards the creature. I had no idea what I was supposed to say, but I remembered Reverie's admonition to believe in the magic, so I grabbed a handful of the lava burning inside my chest and yelled, "Be gone, you stinking dirt bag!"

For the briefest of seconds nothing happened, and I knew I had failed, but then the outlines of the creature began to blur and fade. It dissolved into smoke and blew away on the wind.

"Stinking dirt bag?" snickered Allegra, now returned to her human form. She shook her head and snorted. "Witches and their flair for the dramatic."

I giggled hysterically. Her comment helped to ease the tension just a tad, but Allegra noticed how badly I was quivering.

"Sit down before you fall down," she commanded. I obeyed immediately.

"What was that?" I asked shakily as she pushed my head between my knees and ordered me to take deep breaths as I sat on the curb.

"A Skinwalker, the shade of a dead shaman, or in this case, a dead Warlock who practiced black magic. You can only destroy them by speaking their true name."

"Was it Jasper Finch?" I guessed.

"Probably. To become a Skinwalker, among other things, the practitioner must kill a family member, the worst sacrilege known to a Native American medicine man. We know Jasper murdered his father."

"I thought he was dead! Is a shade like a ghost?" I queried as I clenched my fist, willing my hands to stop shaking.

"Similar, but more substantial and much more dangerous. A Skinwalker is dead, and he can't travel far from the place of his death, but his spirit can possess carcasses for a short time until the highjacked body decomposes. It is dark magic of the worst kind. So, tell me, what brought the wrath of a Yee Naaldlooshii upon you? I saw you bolt out of the shop like it was a burning building. I asked Briar, and she said you had discovered something, so I followed."

"It's a good thing you did, or I would be toast now." My need to get the key safely home resumed, and I decided I was recovered enough to continue, so I stood. "Yesterday, the pikas and I discovered a secret compartment in a wooden column Lorelei had given to Ric. The keyhole was hidden behind a nameplate engraved with the name Alaric on it, but Ric didn't realize it existed and didn't know of a key. I just found a key hidden by a Witch's spell in the decorative metal planter Briar keeps at the shop to hold the bonsai. It was given to her by Lorelei." I held the key out in my flat palm for her to inspect.

"Well, what are you waiting for? I think we need to get home." She returned to her fox form and streaked ahead of me.

What if the Skinwalker returned? Thanks to Allegra, I knew the banishment I had performed was not permanent. Great, I was left alone again! I shot after her, casting fearful sidelong glances into the shadows, and almost jumping out of my skin when my heavy breathing and clumsy footfalls startled a deer, and it bolted deeper into the woods. I had stumbled about a hundred yards up the steep lane when a contingency of Pixies with swords drawn flanked me. I openly flinched, the emotional fear and physical strain were obviously taking their toll.

"Caretaker, we will escort you home," offered the lead male, Cormac, maybe? It was hard to tell them apart. I had no doubt those piercingly sharp little swords and spears could wreak substantial damage, maybe even death, if shoved forcefully enough into unsuspecting eyes or ears. This fact relieved my anxiety marginally.

"How did you know I might need protection?" I asked while gasping for breath.

"Allegra, in fox form, can communicate with all the forest animals, a message was relayed to us by a blue jay." Allegra was a woman of many talents, I thought appreciatively, not the least of which was saving my skinny butt.

"Thanks," was all I managed to grunt as I hurried along, a stitch beginning to burn sharply in my side.

When I reached the house, the pikas were all gathered on the doorstep waiting expectantly. Allegra was pacing on the front flagstone patio. Reverie was already striding up the drive, obviously intent on finding me and bringing me back safely. The lead Pixie gave me a salute as they flew away in a swirl reminiscent of a school of fish changing course in the depths of the ocean. I doubled over, put my hands on my knees, and panted.

Once Reverie had hugged me fiercely, she held me at arm's length and stated, "Allegra explained what she could, let's go see if your theory holds true."

The pikas scurried to the nearest hidey hole while the ladies and I trooped down to the basement. When we reached the bust of Alaric of the Visigoths resting on his wooden plinth, I swung the heart shaped name plate up to reveal the keyhole. I heard Reverie's startled intake of breath.

I inserted the key and turned it; the lock clicked, and suddenly I knew why there had been no cracks to indicate a drawer. The whole front face of the column's cap flipped down on hidden hinges like the tailgate on a truck, revealing a hollow compartment. Inside lay a thick spell book labeled *The Book of Shadows* by Jasper Orville Finch.

We had located the missing grimoire.

Chapter 15

Reverie lifted the grimoire gingerly and began to slowly turn the pages.

"It's all in Latin. Translating ancient languages is fiddly, so it will take me weeks." Didn't I know it. If our experience with the Greek numbers yesterday was any indication of the time commitment, it might take her months to translate that big volume.

"I'll have to start at the beginning because I don't know exactly when he came up with the Curse, and there might be important information regarding the counter-curse sprinkled throughout his notes. We can't afford to get this wrong because we'll probably only get one shot at it. A counter-curse done wrong can backfire and be deadly."

I don't know what I had expected. Well, yes, I did; when I saw the grimoire, I thought we might be able to turn to a page labeled Pika Curse (in English, of course) and undo this whole mess, but that was way too simple. The word pika might not be mentioned at all in the grimoire. Had Jasper even known what my great-grandfather would become? He was already dead when the enchantment spell had taken effect.

"I feel like we're taking one step forward and three steps back," I whined in frustration.

"No, my dear, you can't think of it like that; this is a huge step forward!" exclaimed Ric. From his perspective, having lived 58 years under the effects of the Curse, this was an enormous leap. If anyone had reason to be discouraged, it was him, seeing as part of the answer had been right here, under his nose—or more specifically—above his nose, the entire time.

Reverie studied the first page, "I don't know how much of this I can take in one sitting. These spells are disgusting." She turned a few more pages before voicing another thought. "Oh, and there most certainly will be parts of this written in code, any decent Witch worth his salt would throw in a few coded messages."

"About that," volunteered Vinn with hesitation. "I think we have more we need to tell you."

He cast a pointed glare at me and the other pikas as if to say, "We had better come clean now or pay the price later." We suddenly all realized the foolishness of keeping important information from Reverie. Not only was she our personal advocate, she was the only adult Witch on the Mountain with enough knowledge to solve the problem.

"Oh, dear," commented Reverie as she glanced at each of our sheepish expressions, "I gather this may take a while. I think we'd better go upstairs, get some cake, and make ourselves comfortable." Sugar seemed to be Reverie's drug of choice and solution to many problems. I was in total agreement with this method.

"I need to get back to work," said Allegra uncomfortably. She was abandoning ship, so much for moral support from her corner. "I left Briar on her own without explanation. Someone will have to fill me in later." Allegra melted into her fox physique, and in true fair-weather-friend-form, streaked out the door.

* * *

I was on the sofa in the living room. Reverie was in a chair to my right with the pikas clustered on the coffee table along with our empty cake plates. I had started at the beginning, telling Reverie of my visit to the Pixies, their blood oath with Lorelei, my receipt of the silver bookmark, our efforts to translate the engravings, and accidently stumbling upon the hidden key hole in the plinth under the bust of Alaric the Visigoth. I then told of retracing Lorelei's visit to both Allegra and

Briar, including my fruitless examination of the painting Lorelei had given to Allegra, and how the water charm had led me to discover the key spelled into the branches of Briar's decorative bonsai container, and concluding with my encounter with the Skinwalker. Whereupon, I was once again sent off to retrieve the bookmark.

This time, when I reached into my sock drawer, the charm at my wrist glowed a feeble, sickly, swamp water green, confirming our speculation about Jasper placing an enchantment on the bookmark. I thoughtfully carried the flat piece of engraved silver along with our translation to Reverie and showed her the color of my water charm.

"Well," remarked Reverie after examining everything, "Given the circumstances, I'd say it's most certainly relevant to the Curse, but I'm baffled as to how it all fits together. It does have a deteriorating hording spell placed upon it, specifically keyed to Pixies who have a propensity towards shiny things. Maybe he meant to make a blood oath of his own and entrust it to the care of his hive of Pixies for safe keeping but was killed before he could."

"That might have been his original thought," said Ric, "But he tortured and killed all the Pixies in his family's hive, except for two."

"That's awful," I exclaimed.

"We weren't exaggerating when we said he was evil. He caged them, which is a death sentence to Pixies in and of itself, but he also pulled off their wings and used them in all manner of twisted spells. When Lorelei and I freed the only survivors from his dungeon lab, they said he had even cannibalized some of them."

"He ate them?" I shuddered while Ric nodded in affirmation. No wonder witchcraft had a bad rap in the human world.

"Cannibalism is part of the process of becoming a Skinwalker, from what I have read," added Reverie.

"You say both Allegra and Briar mentioned Lorelei was not herself that day, acting irrational even? Everyone has assumed this was because of impending childbirth, but if we remove that fact from the equation, what can we deduce? Reverie?" Ric asked pensively as he pulled on his ear again.

"Taking into consideration everything we know now, I'd say she may have triggered a booby trap spell, something set up by Jasper to keep anyone from unraveling the counter-curse. It could have befuddled her mind, caused her early labor, or contributed to her death."

"Exactly what I was thinking," mused Ric.

"We know she discovered something the day of her death because she hid the grimoire and the key, and possibly all her notes. Then she took this bookmark to the Pixies and had them swear a blood oath. She was either paranoid or had discovered a real threat," speculated Reverie.

"Or both," I added.

"We need to take necessary precautions. Lyric, you'll continue your magic lessons." I started to protest, but she held up her hand for silence, and continued, "It's more important than ever for you to know how to defend yourself and learn as much as you can as quickly as you can." I relented begrudgingly. I could see her logic.

"I will spend every afternoon and evening translating the grimoire, but this is not going to be a quick process, and I will not neglect the Mountain, my health, or other important duties in the process." She gave me a pointed glance to let me know "other important duties" meant my education. The pikas, who had the most at stake here, nodded in agreement, which showed their deep love and respect for Reverie and her judgment.

"Also, Lyric, you are not to leave this house without me, not with a Skinwalker on the loose. The house is warded against evil, but outside of these walls it's just too dangerous until we can figure this out."

So, while Reverie began the tedious job of translating the grimoire, the pikas and I watched the original *Star Wars* movie sprawled on a mound of cushions in their basement haven. Zeke even delivered my dinner while I lounged surrounded by little furry lumps of security with bright black eyes.

* * *

The next morning when I came into the attic lab, Reverie suggested it might be time for me to learn to make my own witchlight.

"You've already mastered the hardest part, and it's a spell you can practice on your own without having a protective circle. It's the first spell most young Witches learn, but because you had some experience with telekinesis, we started with that first."

"Okay. What do I need to do?" I queried with determination as I shoved my hair behind my ears. Barrettes and ponytail holders were useless with my hair. They just slid out.

"Remember how you used your power to light the paper and the candles in the spell we did for the valerian trinket?"

"Yes." I bit my lip with concern. Control had been a bit of an issue when I had conjured fire the first time. The paper ignited when I didn't want it to, and the wick would not light when I did.

"It's the same principal, but this time there will be no paper or wick to light, so be careful, you will be burning your own energy reserves as fuel. As you do the spell, I want to you to think about light rather than warmth. You force the light out the ends of your fingertips and when it appears you flip it end over end, round and round, binding it in your will until it is encased in a sphere. Again, it should contain more light than heat because there is no outside source of combustible fuel."

"You always flick your wrist when you do it. Should I do that too?"

"No, that's a magical tell," she blushed. When I looked confused, she explained, "It's a bad habit. When we were little, Demelza couldn't focus her energy enough to make the spell work, so Ric taught us to

143

use a physical gesture to symbolically bring out our spiritual power. Mostly, it was a mind trick to get Demelza to believe in herself, but it was a totally unnecessary action, like a magician having to say a nonsense word like 'abracadabra' to make a trick work. She snapped her fingers, and I flicked my wrist. I didn't need the action, but I did it to make her feel better. Our teachers at school tried to break us of the habit because a good Witch shouldn't project to others when they are gathering energy to do a spell. In a duel with an evil opponent, projecting your intent could be the split-second difference between life and death. In short, you need to learn to do it with just your mind, but I tend to subconsciously fall back on old habits, like some people bite their nails or twist their hair."

"It does make it more dramatic," I commented, thinking of Allegra's disdain for Witchy theatrics.

"Just remember drama can get you killed. Now quit stalling, and do the spell," she chided jokingly. "Start small until you have a good grasp on the principles of the spell."

I concentrated on my energy source, and mentally taking a pinch, I forced it out between my fingers. A small yellowish orange flame appeared.

"Good, now wrap it in your will."

I nudged the energy, flipping it end over end, transferring a little of my power to surround it. The result was a small, cylindrical vial of murky light shaped like a tootsie roll. I cried out in alarm, and the whole thing collapsed and disappeared.

"What did I do wrong?" I asked in dismay.

"Add a little more energy, and remember the physics. You must flip it and spin it at the same time to create a sphere. The more spherical you make your ball, the more brightly your light will glow. Try again."

It turns out, mentally flipping and spinning energy is like physically rubbing your tummy and patting your head at the same time.

Let's just say it takes monumental concentration. My next attempt resembled a warped golf ball, but Reverie was complimentary as always. When I dropped the energy or lost concentration, the spell fizzled out automatically. It took over a dozen tries, but I finally had a perfectly spherical softball-sized light floating above my palm, which emitted a soft yellow glow. I realized it was almost lunch time, and the lesson had taken all morning.

"How do you feel?" asked Reverie.

"Elated...and exhausted," I admitted as I exhaled deeply.

"No headache?" she queried.

I considered the question and shook my head. That was encouraging progress.

"Now that you've mastered the basic size and shape, you need to practice until you can conjure it without so much mental effort. Magic is a bit like muscle memory. When you learn to play a piece on the piano, the more you practice, the easier it will become until it takes little concentration or effort. Practice, but remember what I said: Never deplete yourself completely, no matter how tempting it is to master a task."

Reverie knew me better than I was willing to admit. In the past, I had been so driven to perfection in my schoolwork, one of the only areas where I had excelled, I had sometimes lost perspective and pushed myself to exhaustion. Maybe she knew me because I reminded her of herself, or perhaps of Mother?

"After a while," she continued, "you will be able to push your light wherever you need it to go. It can hover over your shoulder or precede you down a dark tunnel. You can make it bigger or smaller, brighter or dimmer."

After lunch, the pikas invited me to watch *Mission: Impossible* with them, but not being in the mood for explosions and implausible stunts and thinking they were tempting fate with that particular title,

I chose to do homework instead. I spent the afternoon sitting in the lab, alternating between reading my assignment on teleportation and practicing my witchlight, while Reverie painstakingly and feverishly translated Jasper's grimoire. I wanted to stay close at hand in case she discovered something, and I wasn't allowed to go anywhere anyway, but without any of my usual diversions or outings to look forward to, I felt stagnant and claustrophobic. Time ticked by in agonizingly painful slowness.

A pattern emerged; I would read a paragraph then switch over to practicing my witchlight. I would lose focus, and my witchlight would dissolve whereupon I would take a turn around the room and peer sightlessly into the cabinets. Then I would start the whole process over again. During the afternoon, the effort it took to produce my witchlight became much easier, and I retained two important facts about teleportation: You cannot teleport into a Witch's residence because of their protective wards, even the Witch who lives in the house can only teleport themselves as far as their own front door; and to teleport, you had to open a pathway through the Faerie Kingdoms called the Everafter. The rest of the chapter seemed like useless historical information filled with unfamiliar terminology and jargon I did not understand, or maybe I just lacked focus. Okay, I lacked focus.

At one point, I became aware of a man-made droning sound coming from outside. As the afternoon wore on, it got louder and louder; soon, it became a horrendous racket concentrated just below us, and I was drawn to the attic window to investigate. I discovered some workmen digging a trench alongside the road in front of the house. In less than a week, the grinding and sputtering of diesel machinery had become a foreign sound to my ears. They were using a machine called a ditch witch, and that struck me as both hysterically funny and fatalistically ironic. I giggled.

"What are they doing out there?" I asked Reverie. I know she was probably annoyed with my restless prowling, but she had too much patience to show her annoyance, and I justified my behavior because I was just so bored.

"They're putting in fiber optic cables. The ski resort is footing the bill. Vacationers want to get away from it all but can't stand to go three days without an internet connection," she scoffed without even looking up from the grimoire.

I had been six days without internet. I could relate in a big way. How long would this take? Would it improve cell phone reception as well? I started to ask Reverie my questions but hesitated because I knew she might throttle me if I interrupted her again. A woman could only have so much patience. I was just contemplating the wisdom of joining the pikas for the final scenes of their movie when Allegra poked her head into the attic.

"They're trimming trees hanging over the power lines and have shut down the electricity to *The Art Hut* for the afternoon. Luckily, they informed me of the scheduled maintenance last Friday, so I was able to cancel all my classes for the afternoon. We closed early. I know Lyric hasn't been out today, and the Brownies say your guests checked out of Fox Hollow this morning, and the next guests don't arrive until tomorrow. I was wondering if I could take her over to look at Lorelei's art collection." Allegra had said Lorelei collected art, but this was the first time I had heard the collection had been preserved.

Reverie blinked her bloodshot eyes, then stretched.

"I could use a break, too." I had a feeling she had stayed up into the wee hours working on this translation. I also wondered how much she needed a break, or if it was possible that she just didn't want to let me out of her sight because I seemed to be a walking danger magnet. "Fox Hollow used to be Allegra's house," she added for my benefit as she rolled her shoulders and fumbled blindly for her discarded flip-flops under the table with her toes.

"Yeah, cute, I see what you did there," I said with an exaggerated wink at Allegra.

"Ric gave all of my grandmother's art collection to Allegra after her death. Lorelei had never hung any of them. They were all stacked in the basement collecting dust. She had amassed quite a few, all on the same subject. Ric didn't want them in the house; he thought they were morbid, and we all know about Allegra's appreciation for art. He felt she would provide a better home for them. Allegra left them at Fox Hollow when she moved in with me 10 years ago. There's not enough wall space to hang them in her current apartment."

* * *

Even though it *was* wonderful to get out of the house, and I knew Allegra and Reverie would protect me, I found myself anxiously peering behind every bush and shadowy patch as we walked. It was my first foray into the open since I had encountered the Skinwalker yesterday, and I kept waiting for him to manifest. Reverie sensed my trepidation.

"I'm pretty sure the apparition was triggered by the key to the missing grimoire. If we are not carrying anything on our person that would threaten Jasper's Curse, I think we are safe," she assured.

"You think, but you don't know for sure, you're just guessing," I accused. Did I mention I could be a brat sometimes?

"Well, we've never had a problem before, so I am assuming the Skinwalker's appearance had something to do with getting close to unraveling the Curse." She smiled and shrugged good naturedly without commenting on my snarky attitude. Her nonchalance encouraged me to relax.

We trotted by the track leading to Elowen's house and turned left at the next street. Allegra walked with the most erect posture of anyone I had ever met, yet her graceful neck swiveled slowly as her dark eyes darted from side to side, always scanning her surroundings for potential danger. While Reverie had a certain spring in her step that caused her long thick ponytail to bob along in her wake, Allegra seemed to glide smoothly forward without displacing a single tawny unbound hair.

I was interested to see Allegra's old house. Most of the homes in this settlement were 80 or 90 years old, some had to be older, yet they all appeared as if they had been built in the last decade. In my reading this week, I had learned not only that Brownies were able to fix and clean anything to make it look like new, but Witches placed anti-aging spells on their dwellings to keep the structure and contents from experiencing normal wear and tear. Modern upgrades still had to be done from time to time, but in this way, decay was kept at bay.

The front door opened into a massive open-concept room containing the kitchen, dining room, and great room with a soaring two-story vaulted ceiling. The wall opposite the door was all plate-glass windows with a spectacular view of the backside of Mt. Timpanogos and a waterfall you could not see from Reverie's home. There was also a master suite on the first floor. Next to the front door was a staircase up to a balcony that spanned the length of the house and was open on one side to the great room below.

"The paintings are up on the balcony landing," said Allegra as she started briskly up the stairs. "They are all reproduction prints, of course, but some are quite famous."

The back wall of the mezzanine acted as a gallery containing at least a dozen paintings. The extensive backdrop for artwork was interrupted only by a few closed doors, which I assumed led to more bedrooms. I stepped closer to the first painting and began to study it. It was of a beautiful woman sitting on a cliff above a river combing her long golden hair. The next painting and the next were variations on the same theme. Sometimes the woman had red hair, and sometimes she sported a mermaid's tail, but otherwise it was the same story. Often there were seamen in boats floating on the river gazing at her adoringly.

"Who is this woman?" I asked as I carefully observed the similarities between each print.

"In Sankt, Germany, on the bank of the River Rhine, there is a steep cliff called the lurking rock. It marks the narrowest part of the river and was the site of many shipwrecks because the strong currents and submerged rocks make that portion dangerous and difficult to navigate. The steepness and narrowness of the gorge caused the wind to make a murmuring noise that sounded like voices calling. In 1824, the German poet, Heinrich Heine wrote a poem where he personified the cliff by saying there was a Siren-like Witch perched there who sang to sailors and unwittingly distracted them with her beauty and lured them to their deaths. It became an instant success, and as you can see, many artists were enthralled by the theme. Franz Liszt even wrote a musical composition about it," supplied Allegra, the self-appointed art historian.

"So, Lorelei identified with this Siren because she felt she had lured Jasper to his death, just like this woman lured the sailors in the poem?" I hypothesized.

"Well, but that's not all," offered Reverie. "In German 'lurking rock' is roughly translated into *lauern lei*. The name of Heine's character is Lorelei. The title of his poem and of all these painting's is the same: *The Lorelei*."

"Okay, freaky and a bit too coincidental, if you ask me." This was creeping me out.

"Lorelei felt the same. I'd say she even became a little obsessed with the whole thing," offered Allegra sagely.

"You think?" I asked sarcastically with eyes bulging.

I had come to the end of the row of paintings and abruptly halted. Hanging in the final spot was a photograph I have at home of a three-dimensional rendering of famous asteroid cluster. Talk about freaky!

"Why do you have a copy of this here?" I asked in amazement.

"After I moved into Reverie's apartment, there was a blank spot here because I took the painting Lorelei had gifted me before she died. When I found out your father had sent you a poster of this on your second birthday, I couldn't resist filling this spot with a copy of the same photograph. It's a bit cheeky don't you think?" She grinned.

"I don't understand, why?" I puzzled. What did asteroids have to do with a Siren on the Rhine River?

"Don't you know the name of this asteroid cluster?" asked Reverie in wonder. "I thought Demelza would have at least mentioned the name." I shook my head.

"This asteroid cluster is called *165 Loreley*. It's spelled with the old German L-E-Y ending but is pronounced the same as our Lorelei. The cluster was named after the Siren in the poem. After all, asteroids are lurking rocks, right?" Reverie supplied. I stopped abruptly, staring at nothing as thoughts begin to whirl around in my head. Reverie and Allegra glanced at me and then at each other, wondering what was wrong.

When my powers first manifested in the flying dreams, *165 Loreley* was the only constant. A different piece of my furniture moved haphazardly every night, but the framed poster *always* moved. We would find *165 Loreley* hanging in a different room *every* time. The ancient Pixie, Cypress, said the bookmark/mirror fell from their wall one-night last January...last January when I was unconsciously teleporting my furnishings in an untrained manner. Back then, I didn't have the finesse or control to shift one specific object so precisely, especially while sleeping.

"You said the spirit of the Native American princess, Utahna, contacted your great-great grandmother, and the Skinwalker is like a super strong spirit called a Shade. Are there such things as regular spirits, like ghosts?" I asked Reverie as I pondered a theory.

"No, not in the traditional sense. A dark Witch can use necromancy to temporarily raise the spirts of the dead for malevolent purposes, but generally speaking, you can't see or talk to a spirit on this plane, and they certainly don't go around moaning and rattling chains like in haunted house stories.

"The Skinwalker is more of a Demon than a ghost. Demon's exist in an alternative reality like the Everafter called the Netherworld. Sometimes their souls can be summoned into our world to preform nasty deeds and occasionally these souls get trapped within a limited space in our dimension, but without their bodies, they are ineffectual. The Skinwalker carries Jasper's conscious memories when he manifests, but he needs to wear the skin of another creature to have a physical body and walk among us. His real body is confined to the Netherworld, so he borrows one. To set a Demon free, both body and soul, in our world would cause widespread destruction.

"I think the spirit of Utahna was an exception not the rule, but sometimes a spirit, especially an ancestor—it's easier if they are related to you—can cross between our existence and theirs to deliver a message, mostly to warn or protect if the need is great enough," explained Reverie.

"What form would that take, exactly?" I begin to move and shift ideas in my brain, adding and rejecting theories, much like I had physically turned and then twisted the key to free it from Poloma's sculpture.

"Exactly? It's not exact," sighed Reverie as she massaged a non-existent wrinkle on her tired forehead. "It could be a hundred different ways, depending on the message and the messenger. If they can manage to push around enough energy, pages of a book might ruffle in a nonexistent breeze to reveal the perfect protection spell, or coincidences might all conspire at once to produce a miraculous outcome."

"Or, something you have lost which you desperately need might suddenly turn up in a place you know you have already searched," added Allegra.

"So, the painting over your bed was here?" I pointed to the spot where the asteroids hung now.

"Yes," confirmed Allegra. "It's the most famous of the Lorelei paintings. I thought that might be one of the reasons why she had gifted it to me."

"The one in your apartment, the one Lorelei gave to you the day she died, it's a painting of this section of the Rhine, but I'm confused. There is no Siren in that painting."

"Ryder painted a Siren, but as his glazes aged, the painting darkened, and eventually, she blended into the rocks behind her, so she is almost invisible now."

"Allegra," I asked still sifting and pondering information, "Why did you decided to show me these paintings today?"

"Funny, you should mention that. Normally, I wouldn't have thought of it, but I met Elowen on my way home from work, and she indicated that you might be interested in seeing the paintings. It felt like a good idea. Dara was with her, and she was the one who told me the house was unoccupied."

Hmmm, Elowen again. It's was Elowen's tip that led to my discovery of the key to the hidden grimoire. Alrighty then, if Lorelei *was* trying to contact us, how would she do it? Well, she might influence the visions of Elowen, her clairvoyant daughter. Or, maybe, just maybe, if her great-granddaughter happened to be gifted with an enormous amount of raw power, perhaps she could successfully tap into that source before said great-granddaughter seized control, and maybe, she could channel just enough to fly a poster with the same name as herself from room to room, or knock a forgotten mirror, the key to unraveling so much misery, from a Pixie's wall after dozens of years of going unnoticed. A small little nudge; something to draw attention back to her, to keep her whole sacrifice from being totally forgotten.

So many things slid into place all at once it was almost as if I heard my brain click.

"Allegra," I said with conviction, "I think we need to examine your painting again more closely."

Chapter 16

The painting lay face down on Allegra's bed as I ran my finger around the brown paper backing. Now that I knew what to look for, I had been able to pick out the fading outline of the Siren perched on the cliff before I had flipped the painting over onto the bedspread.

"Do you have a pair of scissors, or a pocketknife?" I asked abruptly.

"No!" cried Allegra in horror, "I will not allow you to destroy this painting." I took that to mean she had a sharp implement but was unwilling to let me use it on her artwork. I chose to appeal to Reverie instead.

"I think there is a false back on this painting," I said, hopeful that logic would win out over emotion. "If you run your finger along the edge here, the top piece of paper curls away just slightly from the true backing. See the difference between the two?" She ran her hand over the place I indicated.

"Whoever glued them together was in a hurry and used an inferior material for the new backing, probably whatever they had on hand at the time. The pixie, Callalili, who took Lorelei's blood oath, hid the confession of her deception between the mirror and the backing of the frame she had made. Several times, I have wondered if Callalili withheld information to the bitter end, because now we know she was bespelled, and maybe the written confession behind the mirror was a subconscious clue to something Lorelei told her she'd left behind a frame."

"Perhaps Lorelei told her she had hidden something important behind the painting she had given to Allegra, and Callalili was supposed to pass that little tidbit of information along to a relative when the oath was fulfilled?" surmised Reverie.

Casting a pleading glance for understanding at Allegra, she retrieved a butter knife from the kitchen. The Kitsune stood stoically with her lips pressed in a tight line and her jaw clenched. She would not refuse, but she would not consent either. Starting in a corner, Reverie worked the knife gently between the two pieces of paper until the false back began to peel away, revealing a letter written in neat handwriting on two sheets of yellowed paper dated July 17, 1962. The three of us leaned in and peered at it for several beats.

"That's my mother's birthday. It's addressed to Ric. I think he should be here," stated Reverie solemnly. I poked my head into the hall and called for the pikas. They arrived on the double, and we all gathered around to read Lorelei's last missive written on the day Elowen had been born. Reverie, acting as voice, read it aloud.

My Dearest Alaric,

I fear I have made a terrible mistake, but hopefully I am wrong; and if not, you will soon set everything straight for yourself and for sweet Elowen. Yesterday, I came upon a smug notation in Jasper's grimoire stating the counter-curse was a cipher code. The book, he said, was his favorite and the code's key was contained within. I informed you I had made a breakthrough but did not want to share it with you until I was sure.

I made another trip to Jasper's cabin to search his belongings once again. I had been over that house so many times searching for the grimoire, I knew every inch, so I was relatively sure I knew the book, an insipid romance with the code's key tucked inside on an engraved silver bookmark. When I searched for the grimoire, I had actually handled the book and bookmark many times not realizing what I held.

I deciphered the counter-curse, using the simple substitution code, and discovered Jasper had made a poppet of me. *Dearest Ric, this is why the Curse did not dissolve upon his death. As long as the poppet survives, so will the Curse. It will take the combined strength of three Witches to destroy it, and it **must** be destroyed for the Curse to be dissolved.*

Early this morning, I determined to go to Jasper's once again. I had never seen this poppet, but I knew it must be there somewhere. I used a strand of my own hair in a finding spell. What a sneaky man! The grimoire had been hidden under some floorboards and I found the poppet behind a loose brick in his fireplace. Immediately upon touching it, I began to feel ill. I have never had a child before, so I am not sure if this sickness I feel is due to her arrival, or if there was poison on the poppet. At this time, I do not wish to worry you in case I am acting like a hysterical pregnant woman, and all my paranoia will prove unfounded after the birth. All the same, Ric, do not touch the thing directly just to be safe. Once Elowen is born, I will travel as far as I need to find two others who will help me destroy it. First, my most important task is to bring our baby safely into the world.

On my way home from Jasper's I encountered a pack of Werecoyotes who were intent on wresting the poppet from me, but thank goodness, I was able to teleport home and hide behind our safety wards. I have entrusted the poppet to E. I know strangers will come to our home over the next few days to help with the delivery. There will be a midwife, the pediatrician, health workers, and many well-wishers. I do not want them to stumble upon any of this information in case they are enemies in disguise. After my encounter with the Werecoyotes, I believe Jasper still has protégées and spies, even all these years after his death.

I am distrustful, so I have decided to hide everything until I am able to focus more completely. This way things won't accidently fall into the wrong hands. I have burned all my notes and hidden the grimoire in the secret compartment under that statue I bought for you. I have bespelled the key and have given it to Briar for safe keeping. It is hidden in a plant, and plants are valuable to her.

I have put the book in our library and have bound the Pixies with a blood oath to keep the silver bookmark secure with further instructions for you to help you find the other things if you have the need. I will hide this letter in one of my paintings and give it to Allegra. I know she will protect artwork at all costs.

I have called the midwife, but I am beginning to be extremely worried this might be something other than birth pains. I do not feel like myself at all. I am having trouble remembering and focusing on things, but I am hoping all my subterfuge is just a precaution, and soon my child and I will be safe, and I will have my husband back.

All my love,
Lorelei

"She told me she might be going away soon. I thought she'd had a death premonition, but she was actually planning to go find two other Witches to help her break the Curse," murmured Allegra before eyeing me specifically. "How did you know this was hidden behind the painting?"

"I didn't know for sure, but there were more holes in Callalili's story than in swiss cheese, and the current secret keeper told me Lorelei had given something to Briar and something to you. It was the only part of the blood oath that had survived intact. The bonsai held an important clue, so the painting had to contain something important, too.

"You told me yourself this is the most famous of the Lorelei paintings, but it's the only one where the Siren is disappearing, being erased by time. That fact must have been significant to Lorelei. You said she had changed her attitude about herself. She was beginning a new stage of life. The old Lorelei who identified with the Siren was disappearing, and she was looking to her future… Or maybe she had guessed that she was disappearing, you know, dying," I added lamely and shrugged.

"Ric, does this letter sound like the Lorelei you knew?" queried Reverie.

"It's definitely her handwriting, but some of the syntax is confusing. Her thoughts seem so muddled. That was not like her. Her writing was always so organized. She acts like I would know she had hidden these things and how to begin searching for them."

"Maybe she meant to leave more clues, but she just ran out of time?" Reverie offered kindly.

"Who is E?" muttered Ric. "Does she mean Elowen? Elowen wasn't even born yet; she couldn't have given the poppet to her. I don't know anyone else whose name, first or last, starts with an E."

Westley pointed to my father, "His name is Vinn Everton. That starts with an E."

"He wasn't born yet either," snapped Ric in exasperation. It was the first time I had ever seen him loose his cool. Westley had the sense to look embarrassed.

"Hold on a minute," I said raising my hand, "New person here. What is a poppet?"

"Have you ever seen a voodoo doll?" asked Allegra.

"You mean those ugly rag dolls with button eyes that are made to represent a person? You stick pins in the doll, and it's supposed to harm the person, right?" I wrinkled my nose in distaste. If that was real, too, then there were some supremely wicked Witches out there.

"Yes, but a poppet can be made of anything, and some are quite beautifully crafted, but the premise is the same. What you do to the doll affects the person in whose effigy it was created. You would need part of the person to complete the spell, like a drop of their blood or a lock or their hair," supplied Reverie.

"Okay," satisfied with that answer, I asked my next question warily. "What the heck is a Werecoyote?"

"They're a form of shapeshifter, like myself, with a human form and a coyote form, but not so benevolent. You heard them the other day. They answered the call of the Skinwalker. He was wearing the coyote skin, which meant he was drawing power from their clan in order to make his appearance. Skinwalkers take on the characteristics of the skin they are wearing," volunteered Allegra.

"Remember I told you some supernatural creatures live in human houses and some don't? Werecoyotes live in the wild. They seldom take their human form, and they don't particularly like contacting others who are not of their kind," continued Reverie.

"So, if there are Werecoyotes, are there Werewolves, too?" I asked suddenly horrified. I could chalk that thought up to having read too many popular adolescent novels.

"Yes, but not here. Wolves are not native to these mountains, so neither are Werewolves," promised my aunt. Comforting, I thought... or not.

"There is a Werecougar," offered Westley as Reverie shot him an annoyed—you are not helping—glance. He closed his mouth firmly.

"Again," assured Reverie, "She's mostly solitary, lives further up the Mountain in the wild, and prefers not to contact humans or Fae races."

"One more thing?" I asked. "Didn't Lorelei have a valerian trinket to protect her against whatever spells Jasper had placed on the poppet?"

"Well, she did," said Ric, "but it was a ring, and her hands had swollen because of the pregnancy, so she couldn't wear rings for the last few weeks. I told her to put it on a chain around her neck, but obviously..." His voice trailed off into silence. Obviously, she didn't, if our theory proved true.

"A valerian trinket would not have worked against regular old-fashioned poison, anyway," remarked Allegra with a grim look. "So, let's give her the benefit of the doubt."

"Where do we go from here?" It seemed I had asked the million-dollar question. Everyone looked to Reverie, our fearless leader, for an answer.

"If what Lorelei is saying in this letter is true, and we must assume it is, even if it is somewhat unclear to us, then the answers are not in the grimoire. The silver bookmark contains the cipher to the counter-curse; and we need to focus our efforts on finding the book in the library that is the key to breaking the code.

"The problem is," she continued morosely, "even though there haven't been many people in and out of this house since Lorelei died, there have been some, and any one of them could have knowingly or unknowingly moved or removed the book."

Chapter 17

The library was arranged using the Dewey Decimal System which used numbers to classify books into different sections. While there were classifications for science, religion, philosophy, technology, arts, history, geography, and a few more, there was no specific category for romance novels. There was, however, a designation for literature, which housed all fiction and was divided into subcategories based on the language of the book. We weren't sure which language the text was written in, but this seemed the best place to start.

"I'll take the titles written in English since my command of other languages is minimal," I commented as we began pulling about 200 books from the shelves and piling them onto the floor.

There were not many modern texts and no paperbacks. I doubted any new books had been added to the collection since Lorelei's death, but I had no way of knowing if any titles had been removed. I sat crossed legged on the floor by my designated stack and began lifting each one from the pile and slowly discarding them into a separate pile. Reverie did the same with her stacks, which had been placed in neat rows on the library's desk. The pikas scurried about scanning stacks to see if anything stuck out to them, as they could not physically lift books. It would have helped if any of us knew what we were looking for. Allegra was assigned to give a second opinion before putting each tome back into its proper place on the shelves.

"Do you rent out Jasper's house to tourists?" I asked Reverie as I idly flipped through books, looking for something to jump out at me. I assumed the house belonged to her.

"No, it's where Elowen lives." At the look of shock on my face, she continued, "It has been thoroughly searched and magically cleansed a number of times. It's private and remote; she needs that aspect." Huh, I guess Jasper had needed a private and remote place, so he could hide the body of his murdered father and then torture and devour innocent Pixies without drawing attention.

Zeke came stomping in just as the disorder reached a pinnacle. Books were scattered on every available surface.

"Oh, sorry for the mess, Zeke," remarked Reverie absentmindedly. "Don't worry, we'll clean everything up."

"Perhaps I could be of service," he offered with false congeniality as he glanced about at our total lack of concern for his orderliness. As was her benevolent nature, Reverie took him at his word, choosing to disregard his obvious disdain.

"Yes, perhaps you could help," she said thoughtfully, "since you have lived in the house longer than anyone, except Ric, and you are the one who frequently dusts in here. Do you know of a romance novel that would have been of particular interest to the Sorcerer Jasper that was not here before Lorelei's death, but was here after?"

He circled our stacks and stopped at one of mine, pulling out a slim leather-bound volume near the bottom with one hand, as he effortlessly lifted all the books above it with the other.

"I believe this one fits the bill."

He offered it to me. The book was titled simply *Lorelei* and was written by Ionel Teodoreanu. I read the title and author out loud probably butchering the author's name. On the inside cover was a handwritten inscription that read: *Property of Jasper Finch.*

"Duh," commented Westley. "Talk about obvious!"

"Ah, yes," said Allegra, "I believe I have read that one. Published in about 1935, if I'm not mistaken. The author was Romanian. His first name was pronounced Jonel.

"A young woman named Luli falls in love with an older man who is an author," she began to summarize the plot for us. "After a short engagement, they marry, but she finds he works too much and ignores her, so she decides to play a game to get his attention. She writes some love poems and convinces her friend Gabriela to copy them in her handwriting and sign them with the pseudonym 'Lorelei.' The husband is impressed with the quality of the poetry and falls in love with the poet. When Gabriela comes to visit, he recognizes her handwriting, but before Luli can correct his misconception, she dies of a ruptured appendix. The man marries Gabriela, but soon realizes she is not Lorelei. She is selfish and shallow and has only married him for his money. Eventually, he discovers the true identity of Lorelei, which causes him to have a nervous breakdown. In the end, he commits suicide. Pretty melodramatic, but it was a popular writing style at that time."

"I don't think the plot is all that relevant," said Reverie as she thought it over, "Jasper probably just needed a text that contained the word Lorelei, since it had to have been part of the cipher. Look as some of the actual pages."

I flipped through the book. Every few pages, a word had been circled in pencil. Without waiting for direction, I leapt to the spiral staircase and once again retrieved the silver bookmark and the translation notes the pikas and I had made. Reverie was waiting with a pen and paper when I returned. I handed Allegra the novel and read the first pairing of numbers.

"Turn to page 43 and find the 112th word," I instructed.

"There is a word circled on this page," Allegra offered before she began to slowly count each word. She let out a slow breath when she reached number 112, "It is the circled word."

"Well?" asked Reverie anxiously with pen poised over the paper. "What is the word?"

"The word is 'to', T-O, not T-W-O, or T-O-O" Rather anti-climactic, but it was a start.

"Got, it, next?" encouraged Reverie.

"Page 89," I called out. "Word 21." This time, Allegra didn't bother to count the words she just told Reverie what had been circled on the page. We figured Lorelei had already done the work for us, why bother double checking every word? There was time to do that later.

We knew we were on the right path when the first five words were: *To destroy the Lorelei poppet...* I found it slightly odd that the word poppet was actually in a romance novel, given Allegra's earlier definition, but the male character referred to his wife as "poppet." Allegra explained that it used to be a term of endearment. I found it rather creepy because it sounded too much like puppet to me, and puppets are creepy, especially those wooden ventriloquist dummies, but I digress.

There was no punctuation, but we eventually figured out the gist of the counter-curse. Three beings of power must gather under the full moon at a gravesite and cast a protective circle. Then, using yellow fire, each in turn must destroy one of three enchanted objects found on the poppet, and finally the poppet itself must be destroyed using blue fire. There were some other things I didn't quite comprehend, but Reverie and Allegra seemed to understand perfectly, so I wasn't too worried.

"Beings of power is code for Witch. I'm sure he had to improvise because he was somewhat limited by the text he chose. Likewise, there are more sophisticated words for yellow fire and blue fire, but he didn't have access to those words using this particular novel. Yellow fire is what we use for making our witchlight."

While Allegra was busy shelving the remainder of the books we had dumped into the floor and Reverie and the pikas were discussing when the next full moon occurred, I noticed Zeke had disappeared again. When had he gone? There was something very odd about the behavior of that Brownie. Then I remembered something tremendously important, two things actually, things everyone in the room had overlooked, and I stole quietly away and down to Zeke's quarters.

His door was ajar, but I rapped anyway, and it swung open from the simple force of my knock. The little man was perched on the edge of his bed with his head in his hands. He seemed grief-stricken. I crept forward and sat gently beside him. Then I glanced at his collection of porcelain figurines arranged lovingly in the curio cabinet across from us to confirm one of my suspicions.

"Zeke?" I asked cautiously. "Where did you get all those fairy tale princess figurines?"

"I've had one of them for a very long time." He cast me a knowing look that served to strengthen what I had already guessed. I could tell he was conflicted, but he decided to plunge ahead. "Demelza saw how much I adored it, and she began to send me other princesses the year after she left home. She orders them online, and they are delivered to me every year for Christmas." He stared into the distance with a bittersweet smile upon his lips. Instinctively, I knew I needed to tread lightly. Maybe if I could get him talking about something else this would be easier for him.

"Reverie says you have been with her family for over 90 years. How did you first come to this area?" I asked.

"Brownies have always served the Fae. We came with Mr. Finnick from Great Britain to America on a ship in the 1850s. I was just a boy then. He had a mansion in the old country, and a dozen of my family who served him chose to come with him instead of going to other families. When he first came to Utah, we lived in the Provo Valley, and he had a small summer cabin here on the Mountain. Your ancestors had already settled here. They were three brothers, triplets, very rare in Witching families, and each received 160 acres of land from the government in the Homestead Act. By the early 1900s, they owned 2,200 acres where they raised sheep and cattle.

"When Finnick first started coming here in the summers, there was only a dirt road up North Fork Canyon," he supplied, "There was a railroad that ran through Provo Canyon from Provo to Heber City and back. Sometimes, my sister and I would ride down North Fork Canyon in the horse and wagon with Mr. Finnick, so he could take the train to work. We would wait there caring for the horses, fishing in the Provo River all day, until he came home in the evening. They did not put in the first paved road up to these homes until the 1920s."

"And that was fun for you?" Although I'd never been fishing, I couldn't imagine anything more miserable, especially in the Provo River, which was icy cold from snow melt even in the middle of summer. He grinned and nodded.

"Tell me, Zeke, is Mr. Finnick an honest man?" I still couldn't help feeling suspicious of the Fae Faun turned estate lawyer.

"Oh, yes, Miss, he is one of the finest," he assured me before continuing. "It was the old Mr. Finch, Jasper's father, who was untrustworthy, and later Mr. Jasper himself. Jasper murdered his Brownie servants to keep them quiet about his other activities. Mr. Finnick was the one who accidentally discovered their bodies and figured out what Mr. Jasper was up to. He sounded the alarm against Jasper. That was the final straw that caused the Witches to take sides against him."

I figured Brownies would be great judges of character. They lived with the same families for decades and popped in and out of their houses virtually unnoticed. After a while, I suppose you would disregard their stealthy presence and give them a good view of your true nature.

"When Lorelei was born in 1924, I left Mr. Finnick and came to work fulltime for her mother and father. Lorelei was my charge. Brownies love children, and she was such a sweet child. Her father,

Stewart, opened the first ski resort here in 1944. Hilda, her mother, owned and operated a small café at the resort; by then, your family owned almost 4,000 acres.

"There were half a dozen or more Witching families who lived here, and they all pitched in to help at the resort. Some were your relatives, and some were not, but they all lived in homes on land owned by your family. The Mountain was known as a refuge for super-naturals. Mr. Finnick encouraged my Brownie relatives and me to divide ourselves among those families. There were too many of us by then to stay with one Fae household. Brownies are happiest when they are busy and have things to fix and clean. We all help each other out when there is a big job to be done. Mr. Finnick was devastated when he discovered what Mr. Jasper had done to his Brownies. He blamed himself.

"After Lorelei and Ric were married, the Witching families took sides between Jasper and Lorelei. Jasper had stroked their egos and made rash promises about how Witches were going to use black magic to rise and take over the world. His promises were enticing to a people who had been hunted and tortured and lived most of their lives in hiding. He used some of the same tactics Hitler had used with the Germans, unfounded fear, misplaced blame, lies and secrecy. The Nazi regime had just failed miserably, so you would think they would have learned by observation, but sadly, they did not.

"After the great battle, those who had not been killed abandoned the Mountain and set out for other parts of the country to get a fresh start. Lorelei and Ric continued to run the resort for years, and she finally sold it to a rich Hollywood fellow when Ric became a pika and she found out she was expecting. She kept the rental properties."

"Your real name is Ezekiel, right?" This was something I already knew as well. Reverie had told me on my first evening.

Ezekiel starts with an E.

When he nodded, I continued gently asking, "Which one of those figurines did Lorelei give you on the day she died?"

"Oh, Miss Lyric, I loved her so. She was the kindest and gentlest of people. She said to keep it safe until she could destroy it, but it was such exquisite work, so like her, so painfully beautiful. She gave it to me and sent me away because she didn't want it near the house when so many strangers would be in and out while Elowen was being born.

"After she died, I wanted to tell somebody, but who to tell? Mr. Ric was no longer a Witch, so he couldn't destroy it, and neither was Mr. Finnick. When Elowen returned, she was useless," he bobbed his head and added hastily, "Beg pardon, Miss."

I shrugged. His statement was harsh, but I wouldn't choose this time to argue with his assessment. I was starting to see that Elowen was far from useless. She just had different strengths.

He continued defensively, "I was keeping it safe, and I wasn't hurting anyone; besides it was the only thing I had left of her." *Wasn't hurting anyone?* I thought angrily. What about Ric, Westley and my father? What about me, Reverie, Elowen, and Mother? I was beginning to wonder if he were not under some enchantment himself. There had been so much miscommunication, and so many secrets, if any of them had been revealed, it could have unraveled this whole charade. Was all this deception woven into the intricacies of Jasper's Curse, or had he counted on the innate selfishness and self-centered tendencies of those around him to perpetuate his spell?

"When I witnessed your power on that first morning, I knew she was angry with me for disregarding her dying wishes. I knew what you had been sent here to do." *Gee,* I thought, *it would have been nice for somebody to have given me a heads up.*

"I tried to rationalize my actions and hide my deceit. That's why I have avoided you for the last week. I didn't want you to take her away."

By her, I assumed he meant the figurine Lorelei had entrusted into his care. I had to admit, it was an obsession that wreaked of enchantment.

He hopped from the bed in resignation and crossed to the cabinet where Cinderella, Belle, Aurora, Jasmine, and others all stood poised in various porcelain poses. He pointed to the figure in the most prominent position. She was front and center on the middle shelf with all the other dolls turned slightly towards her to show their obeisance. She was lying on a white tufted satin quilt, in a glass box with no lid. Her eyes were closed, highlighting her long black lashes against her snow-white skin and ruby red lips. She wore a long, white silk dress with a white corset over the bodice embroidered in golden thread, embellished with multi-colored jewels, and fastened with golden laces. Her curling ebony hair had a life-like sheen and was adorned with a golden comb at the crown. In her perfectly formed hand was a small golden apple with one tiny bite missing, but this was not the legendary Snow White.

This was an image of Lorelei Killian Noble.

Chapter 18

Reverie, Allegra, and the pikas all had joined Zeke and me in a semicircle around his curio cabinet after I had sprinted half-way up the basement stairs and yelled, "Hey, guys? I think there's something you need to see down here."

Westley whistled, "So, it's been here all along, How about that?" I'd discovered he had a certain propensity for stating the obvious.

"The moon will be full on Thursday night," remarked Reverie solemnly, looking directly at me. "I think I should call Demelza home, and I need to teach you how to make blue fire."

"Wait," I interrupted. This was already Tuesday. "Okay, I think you are stretching it a bit to think I could do this. I haven't even perfected my witchlight yet, and aren't you forgetting that we need three Witches? You said Mother doesn't have the necessary power."

"Oh, Demelza isn't taking part in the counter-curse. Elowen will be the third," clarified Reverie.

"You have got to be kidding. Is that wise?" I squinted my eyes at her. Yes, Elowen had her strengths, but was she reliable enough to be given a responsibility of this magnitude?

"She's powerful enough and motivated," said Westley in her defense, "and you can do this kid, no doubt."

Reverie and the others nodded their agreement.

I shrugged, "You are the adults, but we don't really know which three objects we're supposed to destroy before we get rid of the poppet."

"I might be able to help with that," volunteered Allegra, who had been deep in thought as she studied the poppet. "In the original Grimm's fairy tale of Snow White, the wicked queen, while disguised as a peddler, tried to kill the princess three times. She laced her corset too tight and suffocated her. She combed her scalp with a poisonous comb, and she gave her the bad apple. All three of the attempts were eventually foiled by the Dwarfs. There was a prince, but no kissing was involved." She indicated the items found on the poppet. "We have a corset, comb and apple here."

The elements in play all started to make sense, an enchanted mirror, a lovely princess, a jealous evil character, and poisoned implements to carry out the beautiful princess's destruction. Jasper had knowingly or unknowingly included all the basics of the fairy tale. I'm sure he had only ever read the Grimm's version, so that gave us further clues to unravel his deceptions.

"I'm going to try and reach Demelza in Tokyo," commented Reverie suddenly, probably having drawn the same conclusions I had just reached. She glanced at her watch and did some quick calculations. "With the time change, I might be able to reach her before she leaves for work. Allegra, will you take Westley and try to talk to Elowen?"

"Certainly." The Kitsune melted into her fox shape and sprawled upon the floor. Westley climbed on her back and held onto her fur with his tiny clawed feet before she vanished from the room. Vinn decided to accompany Reverie to the telephone, and Zeke suddenly thought it might be a good time to start dinner.

I was left staring into the face of the one person who would not get someone important returned to them if this all came to fruition. Ric stood gazing wistfully at the effigy of his lost love. To divert him from his melancholy, I asked a question.

"Zeke acted very strange when he talked about the poppet. Do you think it was enchanted like the silver bookmark?"

"I don't know. Hold your water charm next to it, but be careful not to touch the doll," he instructed.

I lifted Ric up on my shoulder so he could get a good view. Then I opened the curio cabinet and moved my wrist close to the effigy of Lorelei. The water in the vial glowed the same sickly swamp green as it had with the bookmark.

"It's probably showing the residual magic from the Curse, but I'd say the poppet has the same hording spell on it as the bookmark. The smaller Fae are very vulnerable to that type of spell. It would cause Zeke to be extremely protective of the poppet. The thought of destroying it would cause him to have unbearable anxiety." He stopped and sniffed, "Can you move me closer? Put me on the shelf by the figurine."

I did as he asked. He crept closer and sniffed the face of the poppet. He shook his head sadly and spat out vehemently, "He used a drop of Lorelei's blood to complete the spell. I don't know how he got it, but he has used it to paint her lips. That's just disgusting."

"Walk me through the counter spell," I asked, gently trying to alleviate the sorrow caused by this careless desecration of his loved one. "Why do we have to do it during the full moon?"

"Spells are most powerful when crafted during the full moon. Jasper probably created the poppet at that time of the month, and in order to dismantle the Curse, it will be most effective to do it at that time, too. We're fortunate that this coming full moon will be the closest one to the summer solstice, the longest day of the year, which will give you more power and a greater chance of breaking the Curse."

"Why do you suppose he bothered to write down the counter-curse? Wouldn't it have wreaked more havoc if there was no record of how to undo the spell?"

"Yes, of course, it would have been more vindictive for him to go to his grave carrying the remedy with him, and in a way, he did. He was such a smug conceited devil. He assumed he would win, and he might need the counter-curse when he had killed me and claimed Lorelei for his own."

"But why write it down at all? Surely he knew how to undo his own spell."

"Are you familiar with the term sociopath?"

From what I remembered, those with sociopathic tendencies have an antisocial personality disorder that manifests in a grandiose sense of self. They are hostile, domineering, and manipulative. They are incapable of love or remorse, lack empathy, and tend to be secretive and paranoid. They seldom recognize the rights of others, often becoming abusive, and feel justified in their own self-serving behaviors.

"To Jasper, it was all a game with clues only he would understand, and Lorelei was the prize. He didn't really care for her, or he wouldn't have wanted to hurt her the way he did. The cipher, the poppet, the Curse itself, it was all a way to outsmart us. Writing it down was his way of taunting us. He did it to prove his superiority to himself. You can't think of Jasper as you would a normal individual."

I stood, thinking for a while before I brought up a subject I had been deliberating for some time. I was hoping Ric could help me gain perspective since he seemed to have some wisdom about what motivated the behavior of others.

"Ric," I asked seriously, "why do you suppose Mother never brought me here to visit my father?"

I appreciated that he contemplated the question for several seconds before he answered, but I was surprised when he presented his thoughts in just one word.

"Fear," he stated.

"Fear of what?" I queried in disbelief.

"Fear that knowledge of the Curse and who your father really was would bring about psychological damage like it had in her own mother." He let his statement sink in for a few beats before he continued, "Fear that the call of the Mountain would be too strong, and your powers would manifest, and she would lose you."

This was something else I had never considered. Mother loved me, and she wanted me to live with her, not here with Reverie. Because Mother could not help me with my magical abilities, did it make her feel like she had failed me as a parent?

"Fear that she was not powerful enough to protect you from the dangerous aspects of magic you might encounter in this environment." This was something else I was coming to realize. Magic was not just the thrill of completing a spell or the wonders of the Pixie hive. It was Skinwalkers and Werecoyotes and other threatening things. Ric's insights gave me much to think about.

Reverie called from the top of the stairs, and when I ascended, she informed me she had reached Mother, who was on her way to the airport to take the next flight to Salt Lake City. If she made the flight, she would be here by late tomorrow night.

With gloved hands, Reverie removed the poppet to her lab and placed it in a protective circle. This served two purposes. It disrupted the hording spell, which alleviated Zeke's anxiety over the coming destruction of the doll and assured everyone the poppet would stay put until we were ready to deal with it since no one could break the magical barrier except Reverie.

We ate dinner in tense and resigned silence. Westley and Allegra had not returned yet. Reverie and I determined to regroup in the morning to start my training on how to make blue fire. The pikas were given the assignment of double checking the cipher to make sure that every word on each page had been counted and recorded correctly.

* * *

When I entered the attic the next day, I found Reverie standing in front of her wood burning stove in deep contemplation. She was rubbing her forehead with a worried expression in her eyes.

"Hello? Why are you staring at the stove?"

"Oh," she jumped, obviously startled. "I didn't hear you come up."

She shook herself from her thoughts and focused her attention on me. "Usually we practice blue fire, or dragonfire as we call it, outside. It takes a tremendous amount of energy and can be highly volatile, and unpredictable, but with the Skinwalker out there looking for anything having to do with the counter-curse, I don't think we can chance doing this outside. We'd just be opening ourselves up for attack.

"While the witchlight is a benevolent spell, dragonfire is a weapon and can be used for destruction. It is extremely advanced magic, and I am skipping several important steps in your training to teach this to you. You can't put a protective circle around the stove because not only does the circle keep anything from interfering from the outside, but it keeps your spell contained within."

"Why would that be a problem?"

"Dragonfire is fire, and where there is combustion, there will be smoke, especially from someone who has never done the spell. If you can get the fire to burn fast and hot it won't create much smoke, but with your inexperience, I can't take that chance. The smoke you create needs to escape out of the stovepipe. If you put up a protective circle, the smoke will be trapped inside, and you might suffocate."

"Yep, that would be a problem," I admitted.

"So, we have to do this inside in an enclosed space without a protective circle, and it makes me nervous. Any number of things could go wrong." Up until this point, Reverie had been nothing but supportive and encouraging about my magical abilities. Her lack of confidence was disconcerting to say the least, but I had to respect the fact that she was not willing to sugarcoat the danger.

"Where do I start?" I asked with resignation as I felt sweat began to form in my palms.

She lifted the latch and swung open the black cast iron door of the pot belly stove. Inside, she had wadded up a bunch of old newspaper. On the floor beside her, well back from the stove, was a stack of small kindling, a larger stack of firewood, a bucket of sand, and a kitchen fire extinguisher. She handed me a leather apron and protective eyewear like Poloma Tram had been wearing at the forge the other day. Reverie donned similar equipment. I'm sure we made a ridiculously comical picture, and if I hadn't been so nervous, I might have giggled.

"Okay, I know I told you yesterday you shouldn't need gestures to preform magic, but as of yet, I have never encountered any Witches powerful enough to do this spell without pointing toward what they want to burn, so point your finger at the newspaper and send your energy towards it. The tricky thing is, you will need a lot of energy and a pinpoint laser focus at the same time." She licked her lips and took up the fire extinguisher in a defensive pose.

I took a deep breath to center myself and then hurled my hand forward and released my energy. A perfectly formed witchlight sprouted from the ends of my fingers and hovered in front of the open stove door. It was like lighting gunpower to shoot off a cannon and having the cannon ball fall out the end of the barrel, so anticlimactic.

Reverie laughed out loud.

My shoulders slumped, but I smiled at the same time. At least I had *that* spell down. Reverie placed the fire extinguisher on the floor beside her and shook her hands by her sides to relaxed herself. This helped me to relax, too. The next time I tried, smoke curled up from the edge of a corner of the paper, and a small flame erupted. Reverie immediately doused it with a shovel full of sand. I grinned, but she shook her head.

"Are you using the same imagery you used to light the candle wick?" she questioned.

"Yes," I replied in bewilderment.

"Dragonfire needs to be much hotter, bigger, more powerful, yet concentrated." *Like an atomic bomb?* I thought. *Or maybe a volcano.* Hadn't I compared my power to a lava flow?

This time, I reached inside and grabbed more power than I ever had before and launched it at the inside of the stove. The rebound of power threw me backwards off my feet; I saw fire spray the outside of the stove and engulf the wall behind. Reverie grabbed the fire extinguisher and bathed the place in fire retardant foam. Luckily, the floor just below and the wall behind the stove were paved with non-flammable brick, but even with her quick action, the smoke detector began to wail.

I found myself sitting on the ground three feet from the stove. My limbs felt weak, darkness threatened the edges of my vision and I was pretty sure I was going to have one doozy of a bruise on my butt cheek. Zeke and the pikas came rushing into the room from all sides. There was now a thick layer of smut coating the ceiling and brick fire surround, sloppy white foam covered the stove, and smoke hung heavily in the air.

Zeke scuttled to open doors and windows as quickly as he could while the pikas dashed forward to assess our physical situation. The terror I saw in Reverie's eyes was probably reflected in my own. The smoke cleared enough that the alarm stopped squawking.

"Are you alright?" whispered Reverie hoarsely as she flung off the protective goggles. I looked around bewilderedly. My goggles were nowhere in sight.

"I feel really weak and bruised and scared, but I think I'll live," I croaked. I shook my head to try and clear the cobwebs but found the action caused a *thump, thump, thump* of pain at the base of my skull.

Ouch! Now I knew what she meant when she cautioned me against depleting my energy reserves. Seeing I was mostly unharmed, the last of her courage gave away, and she sank down to the floor right where she had been standing, wrapping her arms around her bent legs and burying her head on her knees.

"What in the world happened?" asked Ric as he crept close to Reverie's and nuzzled her ankle trying to comfort her. She reached down and absently fondled one of his ears.

"Dragonfire," stated Reverie in an exhausted voice. "I know how to do it, but I've never actually used it. I'm not really qualified to teach it, especially inside the house. It's so volatile until you learn control. We need an outdoor environment, and it's just not possible. We'd be opening ourselves up to immediate attack."

"Might I make a suggestion?" offered Vinn, ever the problem-solver.

"Please, anything," she sighed in resignation.

"The ceiling in our room is much higher than this, and our floor is concrete." Everyone bobbed their heads in thoughtful agreement. I could see where he was going with this, and so far, his proposal made sense. The attic ceilings were low and so many things in this space were combustible: books, papers, furnishings, even the floor.

He continued, "I have heard that Elowen excels at dragonfire." This was news to me, but they all seemed to take this as fact. I had forgotten to ask how Elowen had taken the news about the Curse possibly coming to an end.

"True," confirmed Westley. "It's one of few spells not having to do with clairvoyance or precognition where she is truly exceptional. It takes a lot of raw emotion, which she has in spades."

"The counter-curse," continued my father, "has to be performed inside a protective circle, so we might as well practice doing it that way. In the basement you can make a bigger circle with more air inside.

If the smoke gets too thick, Lyric or Elowen can break the circle. We'll open the windows for ventilation and keep another fire extinguisher handy, but being in the middle of a room with high ceilings and concrete floors should mitigate the potential for damage."

It seemed like a good plan, I thought, as I glanced up at the smoke damaged attic ceiling and felt a wave of guilt sweep over me. Zeke noticed my gaze.

"Don't you worry none about the damage," he assured me with cheerful enthusiasm as he rubbed his palms together almost gleefully, "I'll call in the reinforcements, and we'll have this place shipshape in no time. This is the kind of thing Brownies live for!"

Chapter 19

Reverie insisted I sit in an overstuffed armchair in the living room with my feet propped on an ottoman until I had regained my strength. She tucked a blanket around me, brought a strong, sweet restorative tonic that reminded me of warm maple syrup and my sketch pad. She told me to draw something trivial to get my mind off serious things. I drew Pixies in flight, pikas mesmerized by a television screen, and Tansy with her apron and cap made from a dinner napkin.

Later, while Reverie was fixing lunch, I watched an army of Brownies descend upon the house in groups of twos and threes carrying paint buckets, scrub brushes, and cleaning supplies. As they passed through the foyer, each one had to come in and introduce themselves, ask after my welfare, and *ooh* and *ahh* over my drawings. Some even asked if I would be willing to draw their portraits later. When I chanced to peek into the attic that afternoon, amazingly, I found everything restored and as good as new.

Elowen arrived in the early afternoon, and it was determined I was fit enough to continue my lessons. She looked more relaxed than on our first two meetings. She had taken great care with her appearance, including styling her hair in an elaborately braided bun and wearing artfully applied make-up. She looked casually elegant in her faded jeans, soft twinset sweater, and running shoes. When she smiled, it spread all the way to her eyes in genuine contentment for the first time since I had met her.

Reverie gathered the pikas into the living room with Elowen and I to give us an update on some things she had discovered from Jasper's grimoire over the past few days. She thought the information might shed more light on what we were dealing with.

"I discovered pretty early into the grimoire that Jasper liked to take hikes to the top of Mount Timpanogos as an adolescent to get away from his abusive father. He had a rather disturbing encounter on one trip, so I began to search the grimoire for further references to this encounter, and I found a total of three. I have compiled them and would like to read them to you."

She opened a spiral notebook where she had translated the relevant information and began to read to us:

I stopped at Emerald Lake on my way to the summit to catch my breath and discovered a Spirit sitting on a boulder by the lake. He seemed a most congenial fellow and struck up a conversation with me. He introduced himself as Timpanac and was deeply interested in my person and my life. We chatted like two old chums. I don't know why he was so easy to talk to, but I found myself pouring out my soul to him. He said his spirit had been trapped in the lake for a thousand years and offered me my heart's desire if I would help free him. He said it might be a long and painful process, but I felt a kinship towards him, so I agreed.

It was at this point that I realized he was a Demon. I'm sure I was only able to view him because I was steeped in the residue of foul magic so prevalent in my father's home. I knew Demon Spirits had a hard time manifesting in our realm unless they can cling to a beacon of dark magic. He taught me how to rid myself of my father's influence. His plan was so utterly perfect, simple really. I don't know how I had not thought of it myself, and all I had to do in payment was bleed a few drops of my blood into the lake. I thought I could deceive this Timpanac by partaking of his knowledge and then shunning him, but from then on, his voice seemed to go with me everywhere. I tried to fight his influence, but it was useless.

"Wow, I feel just a little bit sorry for the kid. He must have had a hard life if a Demon taking interest in him was his only means of getting positive attention. Imagine being so desperate you would be willing to make a deal with a Demon. He would never have gotten the upper hand with a Demon. He was either terribly naïve or supremely cocky," said my father. In that moment, I realized the strength of my father's character. Only a good man could have had sympathy and a forgiving heart towards someone who had taken 14 years of his life.

"We figured that killing his father was his first step into dark magic, but I think we were wrong. He had to have known that giving some of his blood to that foul creature would be considered a binding oath, and he wasn't deceived. He knew exactly what he was dealing with," remarked Ric.

"Whether he knew it or not, killing his father was his first step to completing the ritual to becoming a Skinwalker. When he said the Demon agreed to help him rid him of his father's influence, he was talking about murder, but I think the Demon had a bigger plan all along, because there's more," said Reverie as she continued reading from her notes:

It has been some years since I visited the Demon Timpanac. His Demon spirit seemed more solid, yet he was still trapped within the perimeters of the lake's rocky shoreline. He was angry that I had not visited him more often. I have resisted him for a long time, but after Lorelei's rejection, I had nowhere else to turn. Upon my request, he taught me how to formulate a Curse to win back my lady love. This time the price was a greater amount of my blood.

Ric scoffed derisively and protested loudly, "What an egotistical maniac! He didn't love her. He was just upset that he couldn't have her."

"That means ours is a Demon Curse," remarked Vinn thoughtfully. "This information will help us fill in some of the gaps in the language of the counter-curse."

We all saw Reverie's frown and knew she had one more Demon related entry to read:

On my third visit, Timpanac was even more physical in nature than the last time. He demanded more blood from me and agreed to grant my third desire if afterwards I would take a vial of his lake water and pour it upon the Great Heart stalactite in Timpanogos Cave. This would be the final act in freeing him forever, reuniting his body in the Netherworld with his soul trapped near the lake. I asked if he would tell me how to become immortal, and he gave me further instructions in the process of becoming a Skinwalker, but I have not yet taken the lake water to the stalactite. If he is free, will he try to usurp my power? That would never do. If his soul is still bound to the lake, I need not fear him. He is my prisoner, and I will always be able to access his knowledge. If I let him go, a thousand years of dark magic will be lost to me forever.

Reverie ended her recitation, and Westley whistled. Once again, I felt I was missing some important pieces of information to connect the dots. I glanced at everyone in obvious confusion and shrugged. Reverie spoke up. She had a gift for discerning the feelings of others, and a deep-seated need to offer her aid. She couldn't stop herself. Empathy was part of her nature.

"Remember the legend I shared with you about Utahna and Red Eagle?"

"Yes," I said still puzzled.

"Timpanac is another name given to Red Eagle in some variations of the legend."

"But I didn't think he was evil," I stated in dismay.

"He did deceive the princess and pretend to be a god, while Utahna sacrificed herself for the good of her people. We don't really know his true character. All we know is what has been passed down through the legends, and they're sketchy at best. The story does say Red Eagle was immortalized in the spirit of Emerald Lake, so that part fits, but now I think being confined was a punishment. His thousand-year imprisonment has caused bitterness. His love for Utahna has turned to hatred and a need for vengeance. Demons are not born. They evolve from other races; created from the choices they have made.

"So, if I'm deciphering this correctly then we might have a bigger problem than the Curse. We know that Utahna and Timpanac maintain a balance on the Mountain. He controls water and earth, and she has control over air and fire, but I think there may be more. They are two sides of the same coin if you will, light versus dark, good versus evil, or devotion versus temptation. If his body and soul are reunited, and he is freed to wander the Earth unhampered, that balance could be lost forever, and devastation will reign."

"Jasper says he didn't complete the ritual," I stated with hope.

"Luckily, he was too selfish, and he was defeated before he could change his mind. I think Timpanac had such a powerful hold on him that eventually he would have completed the task," she finished.

"Or," stated Ric, "Jasper would have needed help again and would have been forced to complete the ritual to get what he wanted from the Demon. Either way, the Demon was guaranteed to win sooner or later."

"This Jasper was pretty egotistical," remarked Westley as he distractedly stroked one end of his whiskers with his little paw. "I mean, thinking he could outsmart a Demon is brazen, to say the least."

"Sociopath," I whispered under my breath, casting a look at Ric. He heard me and nodded.

"In theory then, if we can undo the Curse," explained Reverie, "We will not only restore the pikas to their true form, but it may also be a way of maintaining the balance of power between Timpanac and Utahna and loosening a foothold Timpanac gained from Jasper in the Demon's quest to gain the upper hand from Utahna. The two powers on the Mountain both have destructive abilities, but together, they cancel each other out."

"I've just had a very interesting thought that might prove your theory," said Ric. "During the years that Jasper is describing in these encounters, we had record snowfalls, blizzards, avalanches and spring mudslides. Many lives were lost. There had never been anything like it."

"Timpanac has power over water and earth, and during that time he gained too much power from Jasper's blood," stated Vinn. "Since Jasper's death, Timpanac's power has gradually waned."

"And," supplied Reverie, "During the years my mother was missing we had wildfires and drought. Utahna has power over fire and air. Long ago, she recognized her own weakness for power and enlisted our family's magic in the role of the Mountain Caretaker to help keep her power in check. Our presence stabilizes her. Timpanac has no wish to subdue his powers. He wants to be free to wreak havoc. Demons take pleasure in causing chaos."

"Obviously," stated Ric, "Jasper opened a portal into the Netherworld by making deals with Timpanac and sealing them with his blood. I think the portal has weakened in the years since Jasper's death, but since the Demon's spirit is still trapped at the lake, he must be using Jasper's soul through the Skinwalker to make sure we don't undo the Curse. Timpanac and Jasper are linked through blood, and the Demon is feeding power to the Skinwalker. The Curse is the last tangible piece of the Demon in existence. If we get rid of the Curse, then we destroy the Demon's foothold in our world."

"Reverie, you said there had never been any evidence of a Skin-walker on the Mountain until this week. How did the Demon or the Skinwalker or whoever is pulling the strings know we were getting close to unraveling the Curse?"

I had almost forgotten Elowen because she had remained so still and silent throughout this entire exchange, but she chose this moment to comment. She turned her milky vacant eyes on me and droned, "Because the third being of power had finally arrived, and he felt your presence, Cursebreaker."

Holy crap! Scary Grandma!

* * *

I was more motivated than ever to learn how to make dragonfire and set things right. It was time to set up our makeshift schoolroom in the pika's domain. We pushed Alaric of the Visigoths and the movie watching cushions out into the hall, opened the windows and drew a large chalk circle in the middle of the empty concrete floor reinforcing it with salt. Elowen had pulled a long, thin, ebony-lacquered rod resembling a Chinese chopstick from her back pocket before she sat crossed legged in the middle of the circle with a small pile of sticks in front of her. I sat facing her. Reverie and the pikas stood outside the circle with fodder for fire as well as supplies at the ready for putting out flames. I touched the edge of the circle and closed it with my will. Only Elowen or I could break the circle.

"So, granddaughter, tell me your thought process when last you attempted this spell." She laid her hand gently on my hand. I tried not to flinch.

"Reverie said I was using the same energy I used to make my witchlight, and it was the wrong kind of fire. She said it needed more energy. I imagine my power as a lava flow, so I grabbed a huge hunk of lava and threw it at the paper in the stove." Out of the corner of my eye, I saw Reverie visibly wince at my description. The cement floor suddenly felt uncomfortably hard and cold beneath me.

"Granddaughter, close your eyes and imagine a flame." I did as I was told. Elowen's voice was low and soothing. "Around the outer edges, it is yellow then it fades to orange, maybe some red, and at the very center it is blue." I don't know if she was doing something to me, but I could picture it clearly in my mind.

"Blue is the hottest part of the flame. Sometimes it is so hot it even appears white, an optical illusion that occurs when all the colors combine. This is dragonfire. Now open your eyes." She was staring at me calmly. Her ice blue eyes focused on mine. I felt the world narrow until there was nothing but she and I sitting knee to knee.

"Dragonfire is concentrated. You must have pinpoint accuracy. It is not messy like a volcano or an atomic bomb." Whoa, that was exactly the analogy I had used in my thoughts in the attic. Was she reading my mind? She smiled and for a brief second, I thought I saw a flame dancing in her pupils. Then she removed her hand from mine, and the world enlarged again.

"It is precise, powerful, and deadly like a lightning strike." She pointed her wand over the sticks, for now I realized that was what she had removed from her back pocket, and a thin line of white-hot power shot out from the tip. The kindling was consumed with flame and instantaneously became a pile of ashes. Only a tendril of smoke wafted up between us and pooled on the underside of my protective bubble. She leaned back and touched the side of my circle with her finger; immediately I felt it fall.

Elowen rose as gracefully as a cat and stepped carefully over my chalked and salted circle. She gathered a handful of wood shavings and arranged them neatly between us. This time, as her smoke drifted out the window, she closed the circle.

"It works better if you can add your negative emotions to your power. Hatred works best, but anger, fear, even sorrow will work." Oddly, she spoke these words without using any emotion, as if she had separated herself from her negative feelings. They were something she kept in a box on a shelf and took out only when she needed them. To me, emotions were messy. They often reared their ugly heads when I least wanted or expected them.

"What about positive emotions?" I asked sincerely.

"Not as effective. It is a weapon, remember? You are not going to be thinking about daisies and merry-go-rounds if you want to destroy something. Now, you try, think words like pinpoint, focused, and laser-like. Gather the same amount of power that you did this morning." I blinked at her in surprise. Reverie took a step back and the pikas shuffled around.

"The amount of power was correct. It was the delivery that went awry. The key is to not release the power until you have the correct focus."

I cast a wary glance at Reverie, and she nodded, so I scooped up the power.

"Point at the wood chips. Hone that power until it has a razor's edge," instructed Elowen in her calm, matter-of-fact voice.

Holding that kind of power took real effort. I had been used to grabbing it and pushing it into whatever spell I needed right away. I realized my spellcrafting had been sloppy and inelegant compared to this process. I felt sweat forming on my brow and pooling at my lower back as I worked.

"Narrow it, fold it in on itself, making it smaller but more concentrated. Do not dilute it, and do not release it until you are sure it is as focused as it can get." I was concentrating so hard; I heard her instructions in the recesses of my mind as if she were whispering them from out in the hall.

The flame that shot from my hand was wider than hers and shading more to blue than white. My woodchips burst into flame then sort of melted into a black blob. My spell produced an oily smoke even though I had used less fuel than Elowen. I barely felt the rebound. Reverie and the pikas all clapped. I finally inhaled. Elowen collapsed the circle again and retrieved an even bigger pile of twigs than she had used in her spell.

"This time add the emotion," she commanded. Oh, yeah, I had forgotten that part.

I gathered the power and started the process of twisting and narrowing it into a channel as sharp as a needle. I thought about emotion. I had been sheltered from many of the worst emotions in my life. I had never known hatred or death. I had experienced some fear when my powers manifested, but maybe bewilderment was a better word. I guess real fear was what I had felt when I encountered the Skinwalker. I was often sad as a child that I didn't have a father like other kids or that I didn't have many friends, but was that true sadness or envy? I had felt insecure and inadequate, sometimes bullied, but mostly in my life there had been loneliness, day after day, week after week of unfathomable, cavernous, soul aching isolation and loneliness.

I heard a crack of electricity, smelled the ozone and saw the white-hot zap of power as the energy left my body. The twigs burst into a controlled ball of white flame then immediately disintegrated into a small pile of dust. There was no smoke—at all. Somehow, the rebound had been consumed along with my burst of negative emotion.

"Bravo," smiled Elowen smugly as the others just stared in open amazement. "I think we're ready to kick some Curse butt."

Chapter 20

Just after moonrise the next evening, we walked past the Riverwynd stables and up the winding path to the mountain meadow where Lorelei was buried. Ric rode on Reverie's shoulder, while Westley perched upon Elowen's, and Vinn was content to hitch a ride with Mother. She had arrived in Salt Lake City in the wee hours of this morning and stayed at a hotel in the city sleeping away the hours of jet lag. After renting a car this afternoon, she had driven to Reverie's house.

Only I walked alone with my witchlight bobbing along to guide us. The orange-yellow light cast eerie patterns into the shadows of the leafy foliage that formed a tunnel overhanging the path. Every now and then, I caught the briefest glimpse of the moon silently floating along above us, and the glow of florescent wings as a few Pixie scouts darting in and out between the trees.

This afternoon, my anger had eased enough that I was finally able to have a decent conversation with Mother. It has been awkward and uncomfortable because we didn't talk about our feelings. She freely admitted she had made mistakes by keeping relevant information from me, especially after my powers had manifested, but thanks to my time with Reverie, I was able to acknowledge she had done the best she knew how given the difficult circumstances of our unique situation. I was left knowing what I had always known; she loved me.

Those of us participating in the spell wore long black hooded robes. Our attire had been the theme of a philosophical debate among household members, but the group consensus had been to dress in traditional Witch's robes for the purpose of the ceremony. Reverie was of the philosophy that what we wore did not matter if we believed in the magic. Roughly translated, she felt it was what was in our hearts that mattered. While Ric believed her theory on principle, he was of a more traditional bent. He insisted not only was it proper, but our clothing would contribute to the attitude we projected. When you dressed casually, you acted casually, and when you wore your best, your actions tended to be more serious and formal. When someone donned a uniform, it gave them the confidence to play the role suggested by that uniform. Reverie deferred to his wisdom.

When we reached the meadow, the moon overhead was a gigantic disk of silver light that illuminated the wide expanse filled with rocks and scrubby grasses. The trees ringing the edges of the field were dense black silhouettes whose leaves fluttered slightly in the barely distinguishable summer breeze. The darkened outlines of the Mountain's peaks rose above us in sharp relief against a clear expanse of midnight blue sky sporting millions of winking and twinkling stars. Tree frogs and crickets chorused in a cacophony of chirrups. The air was sharp and almost cold, which was common for mountain summers, and contained the dry scent of cooling, sun soaked rock and dusty soil. I felt myself shiver and was glad I had worn a sweater and jeans under my robe.

Reverie scratched the outline of our protective circle into the uneven ground with a sharp stick around Lorelei's grave, and then did it again to make the rut deeper. I followed behind with the supersized cardboard canister of salt, pouring it into the gouge, making sure there were no gaps. My witchlight bobbed over my right shoulder. Elowen, Reverie, and I stepped carefully into the circle, and while Elowen gently placed the poppet in her glass coffin on the ground between us, Reverie sealed the circle with her will. I felt a small pop of air as the defensive layer flew up around us.

"Remember even though you can't see it, the circle extends around us like a soap bubble. Be very careful not to touch the sides with any part of your body, or it will break, and we will be vulnerable," cautioned Reverie. It was an unnecessary statement spilling forth from her nervous energy. I knew anyone on the inside of the circle could break it, and those on the outside could not.

Elowen, Reverie, and I had pantomimed the steps of the counter-curse over and over this afternoon. Under her watchful eye, my grandmother had even made Reverie practice her dragonfire in the basement until she was satisfied. Some minute details had been unclear, but we filled in the gaps drawing on the combined knowledge of Allegra, Reverie, and the pikas, even consulting Finnick at one point. Now, we only hoped we had guessed correctly.

I was so nervous, I felt nauseous. The butterflies in my stomach had become stampeding elephants. My throat was so dry, I wondered if I would be able to speak my designated word during the incantation. I chewed my bottom lip anxiously.

The corset, comb, and apple had been removed from the poppet by Reverie whilst wearing gloves, and each had been wrapped in spell-protected cloth. Elowen and I had been given our item before we started from the house. We pulled them from the pockets of our robes now. I was to go first. We decided to destroy the items in the order they had been given to Snow White in the original fairy tale.

My witchlight hovered in the center of the circle, and by mentally dipping out a handful of my power and dripping it carefully upon the glowing globe, I melted a small, circular hole in the top of the orb, exposing the inner fire to the moonlight. I carefully unwrapped the corset without touching it and dumped the contents of the cloth into the flame, while speaking my assigned word of the counter-curse in Latin.

"Perdere." Destroy. We were to each speak our words, but hold our focus, not releasing our power until the last word was spoken.

Elowen followed by dropping the poisoned comb into my glowing sphere stating her word, *"Vincere."* Conquer.

Lastly Reverie rolled the golden apple from her cloth into my ball of light saying, *"Novis."* Reverse.

After she uttered her word the three of us unleashed our pent-up power at the globe. My witchlight exploded into a million tiny sparks like a small shower of Pixie fireworks which lit the inside of our protective bubble and faded gradually away. I had never done a spell in combination with others. The joint power was accompanied by a thrilling sensation. I could see why coven magic had a reputation for being appealing.

So far so good, I thought, as I broke my concentration for a moment and glanced at the pikas huddled around the outside of the circle. They had begun to take on watery human shapes, wavering but not quite solid yet. Ric was a tall man with flowing white hair and beard dressed in a light blue robe. He shot me an encouraging smile. Westley wore skinny jeans and a black turtleneck and sported a thick mustache and long dark curly hair, definitely a child of the 70s. He winked and gave me an exaggerated double thumbs up, as if to say, "You can do this, kid." Vinn, my father, who was dressed in grey slacks and a lab coat, was a redhead. Really? A redhead, was there no end to the surprises? No wonder I had freckles and my hair was not as dark as the other women in my family. His green eyes twinkled when he grinned at me.

Reverie and Elowen had already started gathering power for their dragonfire and were focusing on the poppet. As I inhaled readying to combine my blue flame to the others, several things happened; I heard a wild pika give a series of warning shrieks just before the Skinwalker and a half a dozen Werecoyote, in animal form, burst from the tree line a hundred yards away and began to descend upon us snarling and yipping at the moon.

Startled, I took an involuntary step back, and my elbow accidentally brushed against the circle. It dissolved instantaneously. Mother lunged to pull me from the group and into her protective grasp, but I saw a look of concerted effort cross Vinn's face, and he assumed a solid form for a millisecond and grabbed her shoulders, yanking her back against his body in a tight embrace.

"They can't stop now," he asserted just as his solid body melted into a watery form, and Mother stumbled backward through it. He tried to explain, but once he was no longer solid, he could no longer speak; however, I knew what he would have said if he could have continued. The pikas' bodies had been destroyed when the first part of the spell had been completed. The ghostly bodies were vulnerable and weak, and if we didn't finish the spell the men would fade away and be permanently lost. The Curse would still be in effect for Reverie and I and any other future generation with no way to break it. Most importantly, the Skinwalker's power would strengthen, and the Demon would gain full access to our world.

Crap! What had I done? I knew they shouldn't have trusted me with something this important. I wasn't ready. What was Reverie thinking? I had just ruined everything and disappointed everybody. We knew there was a possibility that the counter-curse would draw the Skinwalker, and yet, I had let my concentration waver. Now, we were vulnerable and might not be able to finish the spell before he attacked and disrupted everything.

The Werecoyotes formed a watchful perimeter at the edges of the clearing, the hair bristling on their haunches as they bared their teeth and growled low in their throats, but the Skinwalker advanced. He carried a knife that gleamed white. Don't ask how I knew, but a small voice inside told me the knife was a tool used in human sacrifices and was made of sharpened human bone. The moonlight glinted menacingly off the jagged, razor sharp edges. The blade was deadly. Any skin, animal or human, he collected with that blade could be used to create a body he could inhabit. I shuddered. He didn't want to just break up our efforts. He wanted to put a permanent end to our meddling.

"Lyric!" barked Reverie, "Focus, we have to finish it."

I began to hurriedly fold and sharpen my power. It was hard not to be distracted.

"Alaric Noble," snarled the haughty voice of the Skinwalker, "You will not defeat me again!" The hatred and anger were evident in his bitter tone.

"Your time has passed, Jasper," asserted Ric calmly as his form solidified long enough for him to speak, "There is nothing left in this realm for you. Let go. Move on."

"Never! I will not allow you to take from me what is mine again! I deserve power and glory and complete obedience from my subjects." These were the ramblings of someone whose mind was deeply disturbed. He was completely unhinged, and it was frightening. Someone this desperate was willing to cross any line to get what they wanted.

I forced myself to focus and became only dimly aware of the events around me, but they seemed to be happening simultaneously and in slow motion. The Skinwalker drew up his arm as if to throw his bone knife at Reverie. Ric gathered what little power he had available to him and began to blink, alternating between a solid form and a ghostly image. He stepped between the Skinwalker and Reverie's exposed back, his arms outstretched to shield more of her from him.

Concentrate! I shouted to myself.

One try.

No going back.

I was back on the basement floor in a protective circle, knee to knee with Elowen, I heard her voice in my mind, *"Narrow your power, fold your power."*

Is it strong enough? Will it be dragonfire or a witchlight? I had to be sure before I released it, but there was no time to wait. The Skinwalker was drawing nearer with every passing second, and soon he would be within striking distance. I felt prickly sweat forming on my scalp and upper lip. I had to release now. At least if the pikas could regain their Warlock bodies, they would have their powers back and could help us fight off the Skinwalker.

Wait! Could I add emotion to make it stronger? Yes, fear...no terror, a churning in my gut, terror of the advancing Skinwalker, and those Werecoyote whose howls sounded like tortured babies. Terror that I wouldn't do it right, and I would lose my father forever before I ever had a change to develop any kind of relationship with him. We would forever remain a sad story of two timid souls who had once crossed paths, neither of us brave enough to engage the other. Suddenly, I was determined that this would not be our fate. I would not allow Jasper Finch to steal one more moment of our happiness. I would not give him any more power over our lives! I refused to be his victim any longer. It was an emotion so visceral, it burned inside me.

Breathe, Lyric. I felt control settle over me. I met the eyes of the others and nodded. We released our dragonfire.

"Jasper Orville Finch," I heard Ric command with authority, "I order you to depart."

In what seemed like a past life, an eon ago, I remembered Allegra saying in order to forever banish a Skinwalker, you must call him by his true name. I knew by completely banishing the Skinwalker, we would further bind the powers of the Demon Timpanac, since Jasper and Timpanac had been united by a dark magic blood oath. The spell that had been the Curse would be lost forever and his portal from the Netherworld would be sealed.

The Skinwalker's arm completed the arc, and he hurled the knife before he simply winked out of existence. Only part of my brain saw the poppet become a blazing inferno, with the other side of my mind I watched in horror as the bone knife continued to sail through the achingly beautiful, soft, white moonlight and with a sickening crunch, strike the now solid body of Ric in the chest and bury itself deep into his heart. The howls of the Werecoyote ceased abruptly almost as if the plug had been pulled on their power, and they slunk soundlessly away into the surrounding shadows.

The silence was deafening.

Alaric Noble slumped into the midst of our broken circle and fell upon the ashes of Lorelei's poppet in the center of his wife's grave, blood rapidly blooming across his chest, soaking his bright blue robe.

Westley, only having eyes for Elowen, grabbed her and squeezed her in a bear hug as Reverie and I dropped to our knees at Ric's side. Mother's mouth fell open in a silent scream, and my father put an arm around her shoulders to keep her knees from buckling.

"Hold on Ric. I can do a healing spell," Reverie encouraged as she choked back a sob.

"I think I'm too far gone for that, my dear," he smiled sleepily, "The poison is already spreading fast, but thank you for ending it. I am so happy to be able to leave this Earth in my own body."

He grabbed my hand and squeezed hard.

"Thank you, little Ricky, she would have loved you." This time I was not irritated by his nickname, only heartbroken. *No, no, no,* this was not how it was supposed to end. Tomorrow we would watch *Singin' in the Rain* together.

"Hold on, you little rodent," I demanded threateningly through my clenched teeth, but he didn't even protest my inaccurate terminology. He only smiled again. It was already too late. His eyelids fluttered as his grasp went limp, and I felt his spirit slip away.

When I glanced up in shock and pain, I thought I saw the ghostly outline of a man in a white robe holding the hand of a beautiful woman with black tresses in a long white dress walking away from me and disappearing into the moonlit woods, but who can say? Everything was so blurry because of my tears.

Epilogue

"It was a beautiful funeral," commented Allegra as she helped Reverie and a few Brownies put away all the food friends and neighbors had brought over during the last week.

"Yes, it was," agreed Reverie. "I know he will be happy buried by Lorelei, but I will really miss him. He's been such a stable influence in my life. His last act on Earth was to sacrifice himself for me." Her voice broke and small talk ceased for an uncomfortable moment while Reverie regained control of her emotions amidst the clinking of silverware hitting the inside of the sink and the scrapping of dishes.

"So, Westley moved into Elowen's house?" asked Allegra eventually interrupting the silence.

"My own parents," grinned Reverie, "acting like newlyweds. She is so much better, it's amazing. He wants to continue his Warlock private investigating services, but it's going to be awhile. He's still trying to adjust to walking on two legs again and having his powers back."

"I know," laughed Allegra. "I noticed at the wake; he wiggles his nose like he still has pika whiskers. Imagine sleeping in a real bed after all this time."

"And Vinn and Demelza have decided to hold their wedding here," sighed Tansy. "Have they set a date?"

"August 7. They both applied for teaching positions starting in September at the University of Utah in Salt Lake City. There were no other candidates who submitted resumes, so I think it's looking pretty good for them."

"No, other candidates, huh?" asked Allegra cynically, "And no magic involved in that little miracle?"

Reverie shrugged and blushed.

"She's excited because she will get to continue her genetic research. Even though she didn't find a cure for the Curse, she's made several important genetic breakthroughs with other diseases and wants to continue her work. They'll get an apartment near the university."

"And the girl?" asked Zeke.

"Lyric will go home in a few days with her mom to pack up their place in Los Angeles and help move everything to Salt Lake. Then they will go to meet Vinn's family in Toronto. Demelza and Lyric are taking him to the airport right now, so he can fly home to pack his own stuff and visit his parents for a while before the wedding."

"And will Lyric live with her parents?" asked Allegra wistfully.

"No," smiled Reverie remembering Allegra's original reluctance to have Lyric join the household, "we've decided she will continue her training and live with me after the wedding. They finished laying the fiber optic cables in the neighborhood, so now that we have internet, she can take her academic classes online."

"Internet, how progressive of you," remarked Allegra with only slightly veiled sarcasm.

"Hey, I'm even thinking about getting a satellite dish, so we can watch live television." Allegra put the back of her hand to her forehead in a gesture of mock fainting.

"Reverie?" asked Allegra as a sly fox smile flashed across her face. "Yes?"

"I have a friend I'd like you to meet."

"A friend, huh?"

"Yes, an artist who displays paintings at the shop. He's from Payson, Utah." Payson was a town just south of Provo.

"And why would you like me to meet this artist?" Reverie asked with dubious curiosity.

"Well, because he's a Witch, and..." she hesitated and smiled wickedly, "He's a very handsome, eligible bachelor."

Oh, yes indeed, times were changing on the Mountain.

Acknowledgements

Separating Truth from Fiction

There is a mountain in the Wasatch Range in Utah called Mount Timpanogos. It is the highest peak in that range. A lake known as Emerald Lake can be found on the trail to the summit, but as far as I know, there is no Demon who lives there. The Legend of Mount Timpanogos has at least a dozen versions. The one I relate in this book about Utahna and Red Eagle is my own slightly adapted version of several of those legends melded together. There is a Timpanogos Cave with a stalactite called The Great Heart, which is said to be the hearts of the ill-fated lovers, and if you look closely at the mountain from the correct angle, you can see the silhouette of the deceased princess laying on her back, arms folded across her chest, stretched across the ridge.

The outside façade of Reverie's home, Thimble Dell, is based on the mountain retreat of the great fantasy artist, James C. Christensen (1942-2017). I regularly passed his fairytale cottage on my daily walks, and it eventually became the inspiration that sparked this tale.

The Stewart family received land grants from the government to settle in the North Fork of Provo Canyon, Utah, in the mid-nineteenth century, but they were not triplets. The first non-dirt road up North Fork was paved in 1922. Brothers, Paul and Ray Stewart, opened the first ski resort in the canyon in 1944. Paul's wife, Hilda, owned and operated a café on the premises. My friend, Kristi Stewart Nelson, a descendant of those Stewarts, still lives on the mountain today. The family sold the ski resort in 1968.

Kilrawk or Kilravock is a castle in Scotland.

Alaric of the Visigoths conquered Rome in 395 AD.

In 1824, the German poet, Heinrich Heine wrote a poem where he personified a dangerous part of the River Rhine, saying there was a siren there who lured sailors to their deaths. The poem was called *The Lorelei* and immediately became famous. Over the years, it has sparked dozens of sonnets, sculptures, songs, and paintings.

The nineteenth century American artist, Albert Pinkham Ryder, has a famous painting entitled *The Lorelei* in the Smithsonian Institute in Washington D.C. The glazes in Ryder's painting have darkened over the years, causing the siren to be almost indistinguishable from the background.

165 Loreley is an asteroid cluster named after Heinrich Heine's poem, *The Lorelei*, and using satellite data, astronomers have constructed a three-dimensional rendering of the cluster.

Ionel Teodoreanu, the Romanian author, published a book in 1935 called *Lorelei*. The plot is similar to the one I described in this novel, but I don't know if his book was even translated into English during my timeline, or if it contains the word 'poppet' or any of the words of the counter-curse.

The American pika is an animal native to the alpine regions of Utah and is NOT a rodent but is of the Genus: Ochotona and the Order: Lagomorpha. They are diurnal and do not hibernate in the winter but live in burrows in boulder fields under deep snow, eating their stockpile of sundried grasses and flowers. They have a unique system of high-pitched squawks to warn clansmen of danger. Other subgenus of pika who live in Asia and North America include Alpine, Silver, Collared, Hoffmann's, Northern, and Pallas.